HIS DARK MATERIALS

NORTHERN LIGHTS

FILMED AS

THE GOLDEN COMPASS™

"Rarely, if ever, have readers been offered
such a rich casket of wonders"

Independent

About the Author

Born in Norwich in 1946, Philip Pullman is a world-renowned writer. His novels have won every major award for children's fiction, and are now also established as adult best-sellers. The HIS DARK MATERIALS trilogy came third in the BBC's 2003 "Big Read" competition to find the nation's favourite book. In 2005 he was awarded the Astrid Lindgren Memorial Award, the world's biggest prize for children's literature. Philip is married with two grown-up children, and lives in Oxford.

"Stories are the most important thing in the world.
Without stories, we wouldn't be human beings at all"

PHILIP PULLMAN

NORTHERN LIGHTS

FILMED AS

THE GOLDEN COMPASS

PHILIP PULLMAN

SCHOLASTIC

www.philip-pullman.com

Scholastic Children's Books
An imprint of Scholastic Ltd
Euston House, 24 Eversholt Street, London, NW1 1DB, UK
Registered office: Westfield Road, Southam, Warwickshire, CV47 0RA
SCHOLASTIC and associated logos are trademarks and or registered trademarks of Scholastic Inc.

First published by Scholastic UK Ltd, 1995
This edition published by Scholastic UK Ltd, 2007

Trade 10 digit ISBN 1 407 10405 8
Trade 13 digit ISBN 978 1407 10405 8

Clubs and Fairs 10 digit ISBN 1 407 10569 8
Clubs and Fairs 13 digit ISBN 978 1407 10569 7

A CIP catalogue record for this book is available from the British Library

Printed in the UK by CPI Bookmarque, Croydon, CR0 4TD

The right of Philip Pullman to be identified as the author and illustrator
of this work has been asserted by him.

Papers used by Scholastic Children's Books
are made from wood grown in sustainable forests.

24 26 28 30 29 27 25 23

www.scholastic.co.uk/zone

Into this wild abyss,
The womb of nature and perhaps her grave,
Of neither sea, nor shore, nor air, nor fire,
But all these in their pregnant causes mixed
Confusedly, and which thus must ever fight,
Unless the almighty maker them ordain
His dark materials to create more worlds,
Into this wild abyss the wary fiend
Stood on the brink of hell and looked a while,
Pondering his voyage...

John Milton: *Paradise Lost,* Book II

NORTHERN LIGHTS is the first part of a story in three volumes. The first volume is set in a universe just like ours, but different in many ways. The second volume, THE SUBTLE KNIFE, moves between three universes: the universe of NORTHERN LIGHTS; the universe we know; and a third universe, which differs from ours in many ways again. The final volume of the trilogy, THE AMBER SPYGLASS, moves between several universes.

Note: the word dæmon which appears throughout the book, is to be pronounced like the English word "demon".

Contents

Part Three: *Svalbard*

Part One

Oxford

1

The Decanter of Tokay

L yra and her dæmon moved through the darkening Hall, taking care to keep to one side, out of sight of the kitchen. The three great tables that ran the length of the Hall were laid already, the silver and the glass catching what little light there was, and the long benches were pulled out ready for the guests. Portraits of former Masters hung high up in the gloom along the walls. Lyra reached the dais and looked back at the open kitchen door and, seeing no one, stepped up beside the high table. The places here were laid with gold, not silver, and the fourteen seats were not oak benches but mahogany chairs with velvet cushions.

Lyra stopped beside the Master's chair and flicked the biggest glass gently with a fingernail. The sound rang clearly through the Hall.

"You're not taking this seriously," whispered her dæmon. "Behave yourself."

Her dæmon's name was Pantalaimon, and he was currently in the form of a moth, a dark brown one so as not to show up in the darkness of the Hall.

"They're making too much noise to hear from the kitchen,"

Lyra whispered back. "And the Steward doesn't come in till the first bell. Stop fussing."

But she put her palm over the ringing crystal anyway, and Pantalaimon fluttered ahead and through the slightly open door of the Retiring Room at the other end of the dais. After a moment he appeared again.

"There's no one there," he whispered. "But we must be quick."

Crouching behind the high table, Lyra darted along and through the door into the Retiring Room, where she stood up and looked around. The only light in here came from the fireplace, where a bright blaze of logs settled slightly as she looked, sending a fountain of sparks up into the chimney. She had lived most of her life in the College, but had never seen the Retiring Room before: only Scholars and their guests were allowed in here, and never females. Even the maidservants didn't clean in here. That was the Butler's job alone.

Pantalaimon settled on her shoulder.

"Happy now? Can we go?" he whispered.

"Don't be silly! I want to look around!"

It was a large room, with an oval table of polished rosewood on which stood various decanters and glasses, and a silver smoking-mill with a rack of pipes. On a sideboard nearby there was a little chafing-dish and a basket of poppy-heads.

"They do themselves well, don't they, Pan?" she said under her breath.

She sat in one of the green leather armchairs. It was so deep she found herself nearly lying down, but she sat up again and tucked her legs under her to look at the portraits on the walls. More old Scholars, probably: robed, bearded and gloomy, they stared out of their frames in solemn disapproval.

"What d'you think they talk about?" Lyra said, or began to

say, because before she'd finished the question she heard voices outside the door.

"Behind the chair – quick!" whispered Pantalaimon, and in a flash Lyra was out of the armchair and crouching behind it. It wasn't the best one for hiding behind: she'd chosen one in the very centre of the room, and unless she kept very quiet…

The door opened, and the light changed in the room: one of the incomers was carrying a lamp, which he put down on the sideboard. Lyra could see his legs, in their dark green trousers and shiny black shoes. It was a servant.

Then a deep voice said, "Has Lord Asriel arrived yet?"

It was the Master. As Lyra held her breath she saw the servant's dæmon (a dog, like almost all servants' dæmons) trot in and sit quietly at his feet, and then the Master's feet became visible too, in the shabby black shoes he always wore.

"No, Master," said the Butler. "No word from the Aërodock, either."

"I expect he'll be hungry when he arrives. Show him straight into Hall, will you?"

"Very good, Master."

"And you've decanted some of the special Tokay for him?"

"Yes, Master. The 1898, as you ordered. His Lordship is very partial to that, I remember."

"Good. Now leave me, please."

"Do you need the lamp, Master?"

"Yes, leave that too. Look in during dinner to trim it, will you?"

The Butler bowed slightly and turned to leave, his dæmon trotting obediently after him. From her not-much-of-a-hiding place Lyra watched as the Master went to a large oak wardrobe in the corner of the room, took his gown from a hanger, and pulled it laboriously on. The Master had been a powerful man, but he was well over seventy now, and his movements were stiff and slow. The Master's dæmon had the form of a raven, and as soon as his robe was on, she jumped down from the wardrobe and settled in her accustomed place on his right shoulder.

Lyra could feel Pantalaimon bristling with anxiety, though he made no sound. For herself, she was pleasantly excited. The visitor mentioned by the Master, Lord Asriel, was her uncle, a man whom she admired and feared greatly. He was said to be involved in high politics, in secret exploration, in distant warfare, and she never knew when he was going to appear. He was fierce: if he caught her in here she'd be severely punished, but she could put up with that.

What she saw next, however, changed things completely.

The Master took from his pocket a folded paper and laid it on the table. He took the stopper out of the mouth of a decanter containing a rich golden wine, unfolded the paper, and poured a thin stream of white powder into the decanter before crumpling the paper and throwing it into the fire. Then he took a pencil from his pocket and stirred the wine until the powder had dissolved, and replaced the stopper.

His dæmon gave a soft brief squawk. The Master replied in an undertone, and looked around with his hooded, clouded eyes before leaving through the door he'd come in by.

Lyra whispered, "Did you see that, Pan?"

"Of course I did! Now hurry out, before the Steward comes!"

But as he spoke, there came the sound of a bell ringing once from the far end of the Hall.

"That's the Steward's bell!" said Lyra. "I thought we had more time than that."

Pantalaimon fluttered swiftly to the Hall door, and swiftly back.

"The Steward's there already," he said. "And you can't get out of the other door…"

The other door, the one the Master had entered and left by, opened on to the busy corridor between the Library and the Scholars' Common Room. At this time of day it was thronged with men pulling on their gowns for dinner, or hurrying to leave papers or briefcases in the Common Room before moving into the Hall. Lyra had planned to leave the way she'd come, banking on another few minutes before the Steward's bell rang.

And if she hadn't seen the Master tipping that powder into the wine she might have risked the Steward's anger, or hoped to avoid being noticed in the busy corridor. But she was confused, and that made her hesitate.

Then she heard heavy footsteps on the dais. The Steward was coming to make sure the Retiring Room was ready for the Scholars' poppy and wine after dinner. Lyra darted to the oak wardrobe, opened it, and hid inside, pulling the door shut just as the Steward entered. She had no fear for Pantalaimon: the room was sombre-coloured, and he could always creep under a chair.

She heard the Steward's heavy wheezing, and through the crack where the door hadn't quite shut she saw him adjust the pipes in the rack by the smoking-mill and cast a glance over the decanters and glasses. Then he smoothed the hair over his ears with both palms and said something to his dæmon. He was a servant, so she was a dog; but a superior servant, so a superior dog. In fact, she had the form of a red setter. The dæmon seemed suspicious, and cast around as if she'd sensed an intruder, but didn't make for the wardrobe, to Lyra's intense relief. Lyra was afraid of the Steward, who had twice beaten her.

Lyra heard a tiny whisper; obviously Pantalaimon had squeezed in beside her.

"We're going to have to stay here now. Why don't you listen to me?"

She didn't reply until the Steward had left. It was his job to supervise the waiting at the high table; she could hear the Scholars coming into the Hall, the murmur of voices, the shuffle of feet.

"It's a good thing I didn't," she whispered back. "We wouldn't have seen the Master put poison in the wine otherwise. Pan, that was the Tokay he asked the Butler about! They're going to kill Lord Asriel!"

"You don't know it's poison."

"Oh, of course it is. Don't you remember, he made the Butler leave the room before he did it? If it was innocent it wouldn't have mattered the Butler seeing. And I *know* there's something going on – something political. The servants have been talking about it for days. Pan, we could prevent a murder!"

"I've never heard such nonsense," he said shortly. "How do you think you're going to keep still for four hours in this poky wardrobe? Let me go and look in the corridor. I'll tell you when it's clear."

He fluttered from her shoulder, and she saw his little shadow appear in the crack of light.

"It's no good, Pan, I'm staying," she said. "There's another robe or something here. I'll put that on the floor and make myself comfortable. I've just *got* to see what they do."

She had been crouching. She carefully stood up, feeling around for the clothes-hangers in order not to make a noise, and found that the wardrobe was bigger than she'd thought. There were several academic robes and hoods, some with fur around them, most faced with silk.

"I wonder if these are all the Master's?" she whispered. "When he gets honorary degrees from other places, perhaps they give him fancy robes and he keeps them here for dressing up… Pan, do you really think it's not poison in that wine?"

"No," he said. "I think it is, like you do. And I think it's none of our business. And I think it would be the silliest thing you've ever done in a lifetime of silly things to interfere. It's nothing to do with us."

"Don't be stupid," Lyra said. "I can't sit in here and watch them give him poison!"

"Come somewhere else, then."

"You're a coward, Pan."

"Certainly I am. May I ask what you intend to do? Are you going to leap out and snatch the glass from his trembling fingers? What did you have in mind?"

"I didn't have anything in mind, and well you know it," she snapped quietly. "But now I've seen what the Master did, I haven't got any choice. You're supposed to know about conscience, aren't you? How can I just go and sit in the Library or somewhere and twiddle my thumbs, knowing what's going to happen? I don't intend to do *that*, I promise you."

"This is what you wanted all the time," he said after a moment. "You wanted to hide in here and watch. Why didn't I realize that before?"

"All right, I do," she said. "Everyone knows they get up to something secret. They have a ritual or something. And I just wanted to know what it was."

"It's none of our business! If they want to enjoy their little secrets you should just feel superior and let them get on with it. Hiding and spying is for silly children."

"Exactly what I knew you'd say. Now stop nagging."

The two of them sat in silence for a while, Lyra uncomfortable on the hard floor of the wardrobe and Pantalaimon self-righteously twitching his temporary antennae on one of the robes. Lyra felt a mixture of thoughts contending in her head, and she would have liked nothing better than to share them with her dæmon, but she was proud too. Perhaps she should try to clear them up without his help.

Her main thought was anxiety, and it wasn't for herself. She'd been in trouble often enough to be used to it. This time she was anxious about Lord Asriel, and about what this all meant. It wasn't often that he visited the College, and the fact that this was a time of high political tension meant that he hadn't come simply to eat and drink and smoke with a few old friends. She knew that both Lord Asriel and the Master were members of the Cabinet Council, the Prime Minister's special advisory body, so it might have been something to do with that; but meetings of the Cabinet Council were held in the Palace, not in the Retiring Room of Jordan College.

Then there was the rumour that had been keeping the College servants whispering for days. It was said that the Tartars had invaded Muscovy, and were surging north to St Petersburg, from where they would be able to dominate the Baltic Sea and eventually overcome the entire west of Europe. And Lord Asriel had been in the far North: when she'd seen him last, he was preparing an expedition to Lapland...

"Pan," she whispered.

"Yes?"

"Do *you* think there'll be a war?"

"Not yet. Lord Asriel wouldn't be dining here if it was going to break out in the next week or so."

"That's what I thought. But later?"

"Sssh! Someone's coming."

She sat up and put her eye to the crack of the door. It was the Butler, coming to trim the lamp as the Master had ordered him to. The Common Room and the Library were lit by anbaric light, but the Scholars preferred the older, softer naphtha lamps in the Retiring Room. They wouldn't change that in the Master's lifetime.

The Butler trimmed the wick, and put another log on the fire as well, and then listened carefully at the Hall door before helping himself to a handful of leaf from the smoking-mill.

He had hardly replaced the lid when the handle of the other door turned, making him jump nervously. Lyra tried not to laugh. The Butler hastily stuffed the leaf into his pocket and turned to face the incomer.

"Lord Asriel!" he said, and a shiver of cold surprise ran down Lyra's back. She couldn't see him from where she was, and she tried to smother the urge to move and look.

"Good evening, Wren," said Lord Asriel. Lyra always heard that harsh voice with a mixture of pleasure and apprehension. "I arrived too late to dine. I'll wait in here."

The Butler looked uncomfortable. Guests entered the Retiring Room at the Master's invitation only, and Lord Asriel knew that; but the Butler also saw Lord Asriel looking pointedly at the bulge in his pocket, and decided not to protest.

"Shall I let the Master know you've arrived, my lord?"

"No harm in that. You might bring me some coffee."

"Very good, my lord."

The Butler bowed and hastened out, his dæmon trotting submissively at his heels. Lyra's uncle moved across to the fire and stretched his arms high above his head, yawning like a lion. He was wearing travelling clothes. Lyra was reminded, as she always was when she saw him again, of how much he frightened her. There was no question now of creeping out unnoticed: she'd have to sit tight and hope.

Lord Asriel's dæmon, a snow leopard, stood behind him.

"Are you going to show the projections in here?" she said quietly.

"Yes. It'll create less fuss than moving to the Lecture Theatre. They'll want to see the specimens, too; I'll send for the Porter in a minute. This is a bad time, Stelmaria."

"You should rest."

He stretched out in one of the armchairs, so that Lyra could no longer see his face.

"Yes, yes. I should also change my clothes. There's probably some ancient etiquette that allows them to fine me a dozen bottles for coming in here dressed improperly. I should sleep for three days. The fact remains that –"

There was a knock, and the Butler came in with a silver tray bearing a coffee-pot and a cup.

"Thank you, Wren," said Lord Asriel. "Is that the Tokay I can see on the table?"

"The Master ordered it decanted especially for you, my lord," said the Butler. "There are only three dozen bottles left of the '98."

"All good things pass away. Leave the tray here beside me. Oh, ask the Porter to send up the two cases I left in the Lodge, would you?"

"Here, my lord?"

"Yes, here, man. And I shall need a screen and a projecting lantern, also here, also now."

The Butler could hardly prevent himself from opening his mouth in surprise, but managed to suppress the question, or the protest.

"Wren, you're forgetting your place," said Lord Asriel. "Don't question me; just do as I tell you."

"Very good, my lord," said the Butler. "If I may suggest it, I should perhaps let Mr Cawson know what you're planning, my lord, or else he'll be somewhat taken aback, if you see what I mean."

"Yes. Tell him, then."

Mr Cawson was the Steward. There was an old and well-established rivalry between him and the Butler. The Steward was the superior, but the Butler had more opportunities to ingratiate himself with the Scholars, and made full use of them. He would be delighted to have this chance of showing the Steward that he knew more about what was going on in the Retiring Room.

He bowed and left. Lyra watched as her uncle poured a cup of coffee, drained it at once, and poured another before sipping more slowly. She was agog: cases of specimens? A projecting lantern? What did he have to show the Scholars that was so urgent and important?

Then Lord Asriel stood up and turned away from the fire. She saw him fully, and marvelled at the contrast he made with the plump Butler, the stooped and languid Scholars. Lord Asriel was a tall man with powerful shoulders, a fierce dark face, and eyes that seemed to flash and glitter with savage laughter. It was a face to be dominated by, or to fight: never a face to patronize or pity. All his movements were large and perfectly balanced, like those of a wild animal, and when he appeared in a room like this, he seemed a wild animal held in a cage too small for it.

At the moment his expression was distant and preoccupied. His dæmon came close and leant her head on his waist, and he looked down at her unfathomably before turning away and walking to the table. Lyra suddenly felt her stomach lurch, for Lord Asriel had taken the stopper from the decanter of Tokay, and was pouring a glass.

"No!"

The quiet cry came before she could hold it back. Lord Asriel heard and turned at once.

"Who's there?"

She couldn't help herself. She tumbled out of the wardrobe and scrambled up to snatch the glass from his hand. The wine flew out, splashing on the edge of the table and the carpet, and then the glass fell and smashed. He seized her wrist and twisted hard.

"Lyra! What the hell are you doing?"

"Let go of me and I'll tell you!"

"I'll break your arm first. How dare you come in here?"

"I've just saved your life!"

They were still for a moment, the girl twisted in pain but grimacing to prevent herself from crying out louder, the man bent over her frowning like thunder.

"What did you say?" he said more quietly.

"That wine is poisoned," she muttered between clenched teeth. "I saw the Master put some powder in it."

He let go. She sank to the floor, and Pantalaimon fluttered anxiously to her shoulder. Her uncle looked down with a restrained fury, and she didn't dare meet his eyes.

"I came in just to see what the room was like," she said. "I know I shouldn't have. But I was going to go out before anyone came in, except that I heard the Master coming and got trapped. The wardrobe was the only place to hide. And I saw him put the powder in the wine. If I hadn't –"

There was a knock on the door.

"That'll be the Porter," said Lord Asriel. "Back in the wardrobe. If I hear the slightest noise I'll make you wish you were dead."

She darted back there at once, and no sooner had she pulled the door shut than Lord Asriel called, "Come in."

As he'd said, it was the Porter.

"In here, my lord?"

Lyra saw the old man standing doubtfully in the doorway, and behind him, the corner of a large wooden box.

"That's right, Shuter," said Lord Asriel. "Bring them both in and put them down by the table."

Lyra relaxed a little, and allowed herself to feel the pain in her shoulder and wrist. It might have been enough to make her cry, if she was the sort of girl who cried. Instead she gritted her teeth and moved the arm gently until it felt looser.

Then came a crash of glass and the glug of spilled liquid.

"Damn you, Shuter, you careless old fool! Look what you've done!"

Lyra could see, just. Her uncle had managed to knock the decanter of Tokay off the table, and made it look as if the Porter had done it. The old man put the box down carefully and began to apologize.

"I'm truly sorry, my lord – I must have been closer than I thought –"

"Get something to clear this mess up. Go on, before it soaks into the carpet!"

The Porter and his young assistant hurried out. Lord Asriel moved closer to the wardrobe and spoke in an undertone.

"Since you're in there, you can make yourself useful. Watch the Master closely when he comes in. If you tell me something interesting about him, I'll keep you from getting further into the trouble you're already in. Understand?"

"Yes, Uncle."

"Make a noise in there and I won't help you. You're on your own."

He moved away and stood with his back to the fire again as the Porter came back with a brush and dustpan for the glass and a bowl and cloth.

"I can only say once again, my lord, I do most earnestly beg your pardon; I don't know what –"

"Just clear up the mess."

As the Porter began to mop the wine from the carpet, the Butler knocked and came in with Lord Asriel's manservant, a man called Thorold. They were carrying between them a heavy case of polished wood with brass handles. They saw what the Porter was doing and stopped dead.

"Yes, it was the Tokay," said Lord Asriel. "Too bad. Is that the lantern? Set it up by the wardrobe, Thorold, if you would. I'll have the screen up at the other end."

Lyra realized that she would be able to see the screen and whatever was on it through the crack in the door, and wondered whether her uncle had arranged it like that for the purpose. Under the noise the manservant made unrolling the stiff linen and setting it up on its frame, she whispered:

"See? It was worth coming, wasn't it?"

"It might be," Pantalaimon said austerely, in his tiny moth-voice. "And it might not."

Lord Asriel stood by the fire sipping the last of the coffee and watching darkly as Thorold opened the case of the projecting lantern and uncapped the lens before checking the oil-tank.

"There's plenty of oil, my lord," he said. "Shall I send for a technician to operate it?"

"No. I'll do it myself. Thank you, Thorold. Have they finished dinner yet, Wren?"

"Very nearly, I think, my lord," replied the Butler. "If I understand Mr Cawson aright, the Master and his guests won't be disposed to linger once they know you're here. Shall I take the coffee-tray?"

"Take it and go."

"Very good, my lord."

With a slight bow, the Butler took the tray and left, and Thorold went with him. As soon as the door closed, Lord Asriel looked across the room directly at the wardrobe, and Lyra felt the force of his glance almost as if it had physical form, as if it were an arrow or a spear. Then he looked away and spoke softly to his dæmon.

She came to sit calmly at his side, alert and elegant and dangerous, her green eyes surveying the room before turning, like his black ones, to the door from the Hall as the handle turned. Lyra couldn't see the door, but she heard an intake of breath as the first man came in.

"Master," said Lord Asriel. "Yes, I'm back. Do bring in your guests; I've got something very interesting to show you."

2
The Idea of North

"Lord Asriel," said the Master heavily, and came forward to shake his hand. From her hiding-place Lyra watched the Master's eyes, and indeed, they flicked towards the table for a second, where the Tokay had been.

"Master," said Lord Asriel. "I came too late to disturb your dinner, so I made myself at home in here. Hello, Sub-Rector. Glad to see you looking so well. Excuse my rough appearance; I've only just landed. Yes, Master, the Tokay's gone. I think you're standing in it. The Porter knocked it off the table, but it was my fault. Hello, Chaplain. I read your latest paper with great interest…"

He moved away with the Chaplain, leaving Lyra with a clear view of the Master's face. It was impassive, but the dæmon on his shoulder was shuffling her feathers and moving restlessly from foot to foot. Lord Asriel was already dominating the room, and although he was careful to be courteous to the Master in the Master's own territory, it was clear where the power lay.

The Scholars greeted the visitor and moved into the room, some sitting around the table, some in the armchairs, and soon a buzz of conversation filled the air. Lyra could see that they were powerfully intrigued by the wooden case, the screen and the lantern. She knew the Scholars well: the Librarian, the Sub-Rector, the Enquirer and the rest; they were men who had been around her all her life, taught her, chastised her, consoled her, given her little presents, chased her away from the fruit trees in the Garden; they were all she had for a family. They might even have felt like a family if she knew what a family was, though if she did, she'd have been more likely to feel that about the College servants. The Scholars had more important things to do than attend to the affections of a half-wild, half-civilized girl, left among them by chance.

The Master lit the spirit-lamp under the little silver chafing-dish and heated some butter before cutting half a dozen poppy-heads open and tossing them in. Poppy was always served after a Feast: it clarified the mind and stimulated the tongue, and made for rich conversation. It was traditional for the Master to cook it himself.

Under the sizzle of the frying butter and the hum of talk, Lyra shifted around to find a more comfortable position for herself. With enormous care she took one of the robes – a full-length fur – off its hanger and laid it on the floor of the wardrobe.

"You should have used a scratchy old one," whispered Pantalaimon. "If you get too comfortable you'll go to sleep."

"If I do, it's your job to wake me up," she replied.

She sat and listened to the talk. Mighty dull talk it was, too; almost all of it politics, and London politics at that, nothing exciting about Tartars. The smells of frying poppy and smoke-leaf drifted pleasantly in through the wardrobe door, and more than once Lyra found herself nodding. But finally she heard someone rap the table. The voices fell silent, and then the Master spoke.

"Gentlemen," he said. "I feel sure I speak for all of us when I bid Lord Asriel welcome. His visits are rare but always immensely valuable, and I understand he has something of particular interest to show us tonight. This is a time of high political tension, as we are all aware; Lord Asriel's presence is required early tomorrow morning in White Hall, and a train is waiting with steam up ready to carry him to London as soon as we have finished our conversation here; so we must use our time wisely. When he has finished speaking to us, I imagine there will be some questions. Please keep them brief and to the point. Lord Asriel, would you like to begin?"

"Thank you, Master," said Lord Asriel. "To start with, I have a few slides to show you. Sub-Rector, you can see best from here, I think. Perhaps the Master would like to take the chair near the wardrobe?"

The old Sub-Rector was nearly blind, so it was courteous to make room for him nearer the screen, and his moving forward meant that the Master would be sitting next to the Librarian, only a matter of a yard or so from where Lyra was crouched in the wardrobe. As the Master settled in the armchair, Lyra heard him murmur:

"The devil! He *knew* about the wine, I'm sure of it."

The Librarian murmured back, "He's going to ask for funds. If he forces a vote –"

"If he does that, we must just argue against, with all the eloquence we have."

The lantern began to hiss as Lord Asriel pumped it hard. Lyra moved slightly so that she could see the screen, where a brilliant white circle had begun to glow. Lord Asriel called, "Could someone turn the lamp down?"

One of the Scholars got up to do that, and the room darkened. Lord Asriel began:

"As some of you know, I set out for the North twelve months ago on a diplomatic mission to the King of Lapland. At least, that's what I pretended to be doing. In fact my real aim was to go further north still, right on to the ice, to try and discover what had happened to the Grumman expedition. One of Grumman's last messages to the Academy in Berlin spoke of a certain natural phenomenon only seen in the lands of the North. I was determined to investigate that as well as find out what I could about Grumman. But the first picture I'm going to show you isn't directly about either of those things."

And he put the first slide into the frame and slid it behind the lens. A circular photogram in sharp black and white appeared on the screen. It had been taken at night under a full moon, and it showed a wooden hut in the middle distance, its walls dark against the snow that surrounded it and lay thickly on the roof. Beside the hut stood an array of philosophical instruments, which looked to Lyra's eye like something from the Anbaric Park on the road to Yarnton: aerials, wires, porcelain insulators, all glittering in the moonlight and thickly covered in frost. A man in furs, his face hardly visible in the deep hood of his garment, stood in the foreground, with his hand raised as if in greeting. To one side of him stood a smaller figure. The moonlight bathed everything in the same pallid gleam.

"That photogram was taken with a standard silver nitrate emulsion," Lord Asriel said. "I'd like you to look at another one, taken from the same spot only a minute later, with a new specially prepared emulsion."

He lifted out the first slide and dropped another into the frame. This was much darker; it was as if the moonlight had been filtered out. The horizon was still visible, with the dark shape of the hut and its light snow-covered roof standing out, but the complexity of the instruments was hidden in darkness. But the man had altogether changed: he was bathed in light, and a fountain of glowing particles seemed to be streaming from his upraised hand.

"That light," said the Chaplain, "is it going up or coming down?"

"It's coming down," said Lord Asriel, "but it isn't light. It's Dust."

Something in the way he said it made Lyra imagine *Dust* with a capital letter, as if this wasn't ordinary dust. The reaction of the Scholars confirmed her feeling, because Lord Asriel's words caused a sudden collective silence, followed by gasps of incredulity.

"But how –"

"Surely –"

"It can't –"

"Gentlemen!" came the voice of the Chaplain. "Let Lord Asriel explain."

"It's Dust," Lord Asriel repeated. "It registered as light on the plate because particles of Dust affect this emulsion as photons affect silver nitrate emulsion. It was partly to test it that my expedition went North in the first place. As you see, the figure of the man is perfectly visible. Now I'd like you to look at the shape to his left."

He indicated the blurred shape of the smaller figure.

"I thought that was the man's dæmon," said the Enquirer.

"No. His dæmon was at the time coiled around his neck in the form of a snake. That shape you can dimly see is a child."

"A severed child – ?" said someone, and the way he stopped showed that he knew this was something that shouldn't have been voiced.

There was an intense silence.

Then Lord Asriel said calmly, "An entire child. Which, given the nature of Dust, is precisely the point, is it not?"

No one spoke for several seconds. Then came the voice of the Chaplain.

"Ah," he said, like a thirsty man who, having just drunk deeply, puts down the glass to let out the breath he has held while drinking. "And the streams of Dust…"

"– Come from the sky, and bathe him in what looks like light. You may examine this picture as closely as you wish: I'll leave it behind when I go. I'm showing it to you now to demonstrate the effect of this new emulsion. Now I'd like to show you another picture."

He changed the slide. The next picture was also taken at night, but this time without moonlight. It showed a small group of tents in the foreground, dimly outlined against the low horizon, and beside them an untidy heap of wooden boxes and a sledge. But the main interest of the picture lay in the sky. Streams and veils of light hung like curtains, looped and festooned on invisible hooks hundreds of miles high or blowing out sideways in the stream of some unimaginable wind.

"What is that?" said the voice of the Sub-Rector.

"It's a picture of the Aurora."

"It's a very fine photogram," said the Palmerian Professor. "One of the best I've seen."

"Forgive my ignorance," said the shaky voice of the old Precentor, "but if I ever knew what the Aurora was, I have forgotten. Is it what they call the Northern Lights?"

"Yes. It has many names. It's composed of storms of charged particles and solar rays of intense and extraordinary strength – invisible in themselves, but causing this luminous radiation when they interact with the atmosphere. If there'd been time I would have had this slide tinted to show you the colours; pale green and rose, for the most part, with a tinge of crimson along the lower edge of that curtain-like formation. This is taken with ordinary emulsion. Now I'd like you to look at a picture taken with the special emulsion."

He took out the slide. Lyra heard the Master say quietly, "If he forces a vote, we could try to invoke the residence clause. He hasn't been resident in the College for thirty weeks out of the last fifty-two."

"He's already got the Chaplain on his side…" the Librarian murmured in reply.

Lord Asriel put a new slide in the lantern frame. It showed the same scene. As with the previous pair of pictures, many of the features visible by ordinary light were much dimmer in this one, and so were the curtains of radiance in the sky.

But in the middle of the Aurora, high above the bleak landscape, Lyra could see something solid. She pressed her face to the crack to see more clearly, and she could see Scholars near the screen leaning forward, too. As she gazed, her wonder grew, because there in the sky was the unmistakable outline of a city: towers, domes, walls … buildings and streets, suspended in the air! She nearly gasped with wonder.

The Cassington Scholar said, "That looks like … a city."

"Exactly so," said Lord Asriel.

"A city in another world, no doubt?" said the Dean, with contempt in his voice.

Lord Asriel ignored him. There was a stir of excitement among some of the Scholars, as if, having written treatises on the existence of the unicorn without ever having seen one, they'd been presented with a living example newly captured.

"Is this the Barnard-Stokes business?" said the Palmerian Professor. "It is, isn't it?"

"That's what I want to find out," said Lord Asriel.

He stood to one side of the illuminated screen. Lyra could see his dark eyes searching among the Scholars as they peered up at the slide of the Aurora, and the green glow of his dæmon's eyes beside him. All the venerable heads were craning forward, their spectacles glinting; only the Master and the Librarian leant back in their chairs, with their heads close together.

The Chaplain was saying, "You said you were searching for news of the Grumman expedition, Lord Asriel. Was Dr Grumman investigating this phenomenon too?"

"I believe he was, and I believe he had a good deal of information about it. But he won't be able to tell us what it was, because he's dead."

"No!" said the Chaplain.

"I'm afraid so, and I have the proof here."

A ripple of excited apprehension ran round the Retiring Room as, under Lord Asriel's direction, two or three of the younger Scholars carried the wooden box to the front of the room. Lord Asriel took out the last slide but left the lantern on, and in the dramatic glare of the circle of light he bent to lever open the box. Lyra heard the screech of nails coming out of damp wood. The Master stood up to look, blocking Lyra's view. Her uncle spoke again:

"If you remember, Grumman's expedition vanished eighteen months ago. The German Academy sent him up there to go as far north as the magnetic pole and make various celestial observations. It was in the course of that journey that he observed the curious phenomenon we've already seen. Shortly after that, he vanished. It's been assumed that he had an accident and that his body's been lying in a crevasse all this time. In fact there was no accident."

"What have you got there?" said the Dean. "Is that a vacuum container?"

Lord Asriel didn't answer at first. Lyra heard the snap of metal clips and a hiss as air rushed into a vessel, and then there was a silence. But the silence didn't last long. After a moment or two Lyra heard a confused babble break out: cries of horror, loud protests, voices raised in anger and fear.

"But what –"

"– hardly human –"

"– it's been –"

"– what's *happened* to it?"

The Master's voice cut through them all.

"Lord Asriel, what in God's name have you got there?"

"This is the head of Stanislaus Grumman," said Lord Asriel's voice.

Over the jumble of voices Lyra heard someone stumble to the door and out, making incoherent sounds of distress. She wished she could see what they were seeing.

Lord Asriel said, "I found his body preserved in the ice off Svalbard. The head was treated in this way by his killers. You'll notice the characteristic scalping pattern. I think you might be familiar with it, Sub-Rector."

The old man's voice was steady as he said, "I have seen the Tartars do this. It's a technique you find among the aboriginals of Siberia and the Tungusk. From there, of course, it spread into the lands of the Skraelings, though I understand that it is now banned in New Denmark. May I examine it more closely, Lord Asriel?"

After a short silence he spoke again.

"My eyes are not very clear, and the ice is dirty, but it seems to me that there is a hole in the top of the skull. Am I right?"

"You are."

"Trepanning?"

"Exactly."

That caused a murmur of excitement. The Master moved out of the way and Lyra could see again. The old Sub-Rector, in the circle of light thrown by the lantern, was holding a heavy block of ice up close to his eyes, and Lyra could see the object inside it: a bloody lump barely recognizable as a human head. Pantalaimon fluttered around Lyra, his distress affecting her.

"Hush," she whispered. "Listen."

"Dr Grumman was once a Scholar of this College," said the Dean hotly.

"To fall into the hands of the Tartars –"

"But that far north?"

"They must have penetrated further than anyone imagined!"

"Did I hear you say you found it near Svalbard?" said the Dean.

"That's right."

"Are we to understand that the *panserbjørne* had anything to do with this?"

Lyra didn't recognize that word, but clearly the Scholars did.

"Impossible," said the Cassington Scholar firmly. "They'd never behave in that manner."

"Then you don't know Iofur Raknison," said the Palmerian Professor, who had made several expeditions himself to the Arctic regions. "It wouldn't surprise me at all to learn that he had taken to scalping people in the Tartar fashion."

Lyra looked again at her uncle, who was watching the Scholars with a glitter of sardonic amusement, and saying nothing.

"Who is Iofur Raknison?" said someone.

"The king of Svalbard," said the Palmerian Professor. "Yes, that's right, one of the *panserbjørne*. He's a usurper, of sorts; tricked his way on to the throne, or so I understand; but a powerful figure, by no means a fool, in spite of his ludicrous affectations – having a palace built of imported marble – setting up what he calls a university –"

"For whom? For the *bears*?" said someone else, and everyone laughed.

But the Palmerian Professor went on, "For all that, I tell you that Iofur Raknison would be capable of doing this to Grumman. At the same time, he could be flattered into behaving quite differently, if the need arose."

"And you know how, do you, Trelawney?" said the Dean sneeringly.

"Indeed I do. Do you know what he wants above all else? Even more than an honorary degree? He wants a dæmon! Find a way to give him a dæmon, and he'd do anything for you."

The Scholars laughed heartily.

Lyra was following this with puzzlement: what the Palmerian Professor said made no sense at all. Besides, she was impatient to hear more about scalping and the Northern Lights and that mysterious Dust. But she was disappointed, for Lord Asriel had finished showing his relics and pictures, and the talk soon turned into a college wrangle about whether or not they should give him some money to fit out another expedition. Back and forth the arguments ranged, and Lyra felt her eyes closing. Soon she was fast asleep, with Pantalaimon curled around her neck in his favourite sleeping-form as an ermine.

She woke up with a start when someone shook her shoulder.

"Quiet," said her uncle. The wardrobe door was open, and he was crouched there against the light. "They've all gone, but there are still some servants around. Go to your bedroom now, and take care that you say nothing about this."

"Did they vote to give you the money?" she said sleepily.

"Yes."

"What's Dust?" she said, struggling to stand up after having been cramped for so long.

"Nothing to do with you."

"It *is* to do with me," she said. "If you wanted me to be a spy in the wardrobe you ought to tell me what I'm spying about. Can

I see the man's head?"

Pantalaimon's white ermine-fur bristled: she felt it tickling her neck. Lord Asriel laughed shortly.

"Don't be disgusting," he said, and began to pack his slides and specimen-box. "Did you watch the Master?"

"Yes, and he looked for the wine before he did anything else."

"Good. But I've scotched him for now. Do as you're told and go to bed."

"But where are *you* going?"

"Back to the North. I'm leaving in ten minutes."

"Can I come?"

He stopped what he was doing, and looked at her as if for the first time. His dæmon turned her great green leopard-eyes on her too, and under the concentrated gaze of both of them, Lyra blushed. But she gazed back fiercely.

"Your place is here," said her uncle finally.

"But why? Why is my place here? Why can't I come to the North with you? I want to see the Northern Lights and bears and icebergs and everything. I want to know about Dust. And that city in the air. Is it another world?"

"You're not coming, child. Put it out of your head; the times are too dangerous. Do as you're told and go to bed, and if you're a good girl, I'll bring you back a walrus tusk with some Eskimo carving on it. Don't argue any more or I shall be angry."

And his dæmon growled with a deep savage rumble that made Lyra suddenly aware of what it would be like to have teeth meeting in her throat.

Lyra compressed her lips and frowned hard at her uncle. He was pumping the air from the vacuum flask, and took no notice; it was as if he'd already forgotten her. Without a word, but with lips tight and narrowed eyes, the girl and her dæmon left and went to bed.

* * *

The Master and the Librarian were old friends and allies, and it was their habit, after a difficult episode, to take a glass of brantwijn and console each other. So after they'd seen Lord Asriel away, they strolled to the Master's Lodging and settled in his study with the curtains drawn and the fire refreshed, their dæmons in their familiar places on knee or shoulder, and prepared to think through what had just happened.

"Do you really believe he knew about the wine?" said the Librarian.

"Of course he did. I have no idea how, but he knew, and he spilled the decanter himself. Of course he did."

"Forgive me, Master, but I can't help being relieved. I was never happy about the idea of…"

"Of poisoning him?"

"Yes. Of murder."

"Hardly anyone would be happy at that idea, Charles. The question was whether doing that would be worse than the consequences of not doing it. Well, some Providence has intervened, and it hasn't happened. I'm only sorry I burdened you with the knowledge of it."

"No, no," protested the Librarian. "But I wish you had told me more."

The Master was silent for a while before saying, "Yes, perhaps I should have done. The alethiometer warns of appalling consequences if Lord Asriel pursues this research. Apart from anything else, the child will be drawn in, and I want to keep her safe as long as possible."

"Is Lord Asriel's business anything to do with this new initiative of the Consistorial Court of Discipline? The what-do-they-call-it: the Oblation Board?"

"Lord Asriel – no, no. Quite the reverse. The Oblation Board isn't entirely answerable to the Consistorial Court, either. It's a semi-private initiative; it's being run by someone who has no love of Lord Asriel. Between them both, Charles, I tremble."

The Librarian was silent in his turn. Ever since Pope John Calvin had moved the seat of the Papacy to Geneva and set up the Consistorial Court of Discipline, the Church's power over every aspect of life had been absolute. The Papacy itself had been abolished after Calvin's death, and a tangle of courts, colleges, and councils, collectively known as the Magisterium, had grown up in its place. These agencies were not always united; sometimes a bitter rivalry grew up between them. For a large part of the previous century, the most powerful had been the College of Bishops, but in recent years the Consistorial Court of Discipline had taken its place as the most active and the most feared of all the Church's bodies.

But it was always possible for independent agencies to grow up under the protection of another part of the Magisterium, and the Oblation Board, which the Librarian had referred to, was one of these. The Librarian didn't know much about it, but he disliked and feared what he'd heard, and he completely understood the Master's anxiety.

"The Palmerian Professor mentioned a name," he said after a minute or so. "Barnard-Stokes? What is the Barnard-Stokes business?"

"Ah, it's not our field, Charles. As I understand it, the Holy Church teaches that there are two worlds: the world of everything we can see and hear and touch, and another world, the spiritual world of heaven and hell. Barnard and Stokes were two – how shall I put it – *renegade* theologians who postulated the existence of numerous other worlds like this one, neither heaven nor hell, but material and sinful. They are there, close by, but invisible and unreachable. The Holy Church naturally disapproved of this abominable heresy, and Barnard and Stokes were silenced.

"But unfortunately for the Magisterium there seem to be sound mathematical arguments for this other-world theory. I have never followed them myself, but the Cassington Scholar tells me that they are sound."

"And now Lord Asriel has taken a picture of one of these other worlds," the Librarian said. "And we have funded him to go and look for it. I see."

"Quite. It'll seem to the Oblation Board, and to its powerful protectors, that Jordan College is a hotbed of support for heresy. And between the Consistorial Court and the Oblation Board, Charles, I have to keep a balance; and meanwhile the child is growing. They won't have forgotten her. Sooner or later she would have become involved, but she'll be drawn in now whether I want to protect her or not."

"But how do you know that, for God's sake? The alethiometer again?"

"Yes. Lyra has a part to play in all this, and a major one. The irony is that she must do it all without realizing what she's doing. She can be helped, though, and if my plan with the Tokay had succeeded, she would have been safe for a little longer. I would have liked to spare her a journey to the North. I wish above all things that I were able to explain it to her…"

"She wouldn't listen," the Librarian said. "I know her ways only too well. Try to tell her anything serious and she'll half-listen for five minutes and then start fidgeting. And quiz her about it next time and she'll have completely forgotten."

"If I talked to her about Dust? You don't think she'd listen to that?"

The Librarian made a noise to indicate how unlikely he thought that was.

"Why on earth should she?" he said. "Why should a distant theological riddle interest a healthy thoughtless child?"

"Because of what she must experience. Part of that includes a great betrayal…"

"Who's going to betray her?"

"No, no, that's the saddest thing: *she* will be the betrayer, and the experience will be terrible. She mustn't know that, of course, but there's no reason for her not to know about the problem of Dust. And you might be wrong, Charles; she might well take an interest in it, if it were explained in a simple way. And it might help her later on. It would certainly help me to be less anxious about her."

"That's the duty of the old," said the Librarian, "to be anxious on behalf of the young. And the duty of the young is to scorn the anxiety of the old."

They sat for a while longer, and then parted, for it was late, and they were old and anxious.

3
Lyra's Jordan

Jordan College was the grandest and richest of all the colleges in Oxford. It was probably the largest, too, though no one knew for certain. The buildings, which were grouped around three irregular quadrangles, dated from every period from the early Middle Ages to the mid-eighteenth century. It had never been planned; it had grown piecemeal, with past and present overlapping at every spot, and the final effect was one of jumbled and squalid grandeur. Some part was always about to fall down, and for five generations the same family, the Parslows, had been employed full-time by the College as masons and scaffolders. The present Mr Parslow was teaching his son the craft; the two of them and their three workmen would scramble like industrious termites over the scaffolding they'd erected at the corner of the Library, or over the roof of the Chapel, and haul up bright new blocks of stone or rolls of shiny lead or baulks of timber.

The College owned farms and estates all over Brytain. It was said that you could walk from Oxford to Bristol in one direction and to London in the other, and never leave Jordan land. In every part of the kingdom there were dye-works and brick-kilns, forests and atomcraft-works that paid rent to Jordan, and every

Quarter-Day the Bursar and his clerks would tot it all up, announce the total to Concilium, and order a pair of swans for the Feast. Some of the money was put by for re-investment – Concilium had just approved the purchase of an office-block in Manchester – and the rest was used to pay the Scholars' modest stipends and the wages of the servants (and the Parslows, and the other dozen or so families of craftsmen and traders who served the College), to keep the wine-cellar richly filled, to buy books and anbarographs for the immense Library that filled one side of the Melrose Quadrangle and extended, burrow-like, for several floors beneath the ground; and, not least, to buy the latest philosophical apparatus to equip the Chapel.

It was important to keep the Chapel up to date, because Jordan College had no rival, either in Europe or in New France, as a centre of experimental theology. Lyra knew that much, at least. She was proud of her College's eminence, and liked to boast of it to the various urchins and ragamuffins she played with by the Canal or the Claybeds; and she regarded visiting scholars and eminent professors from elsewhere with pitying scorn, because they didn't belong to Jordan and so must know less, poor things, than the humblest of Jordan's Under-Scholars.

As for what experimental theology was, Lyra had no more idea than the urchins. She had formed the notion that it was concerned with magic, with the movements of the stars and planets, with tiny particles of matter, but that was guesswork, really. Probably the stars had dæmons just as humans did, and experimental theology involved talking to them. Lyra imagined the Chaplain speaking loftily, listening to the star-dæmons' remarks, and then nodding judiciously or shaking his head in regret. But what might be passing between them, she couldn't conceive.

Nor was she particularly interested. In many ways Lyra was a barbarian. What she liked best was clambering over the College roofs with Roger, the Kitchen boy who was her particular friend, to spit plum-stones on the heads of passing Scholars or to hoot like owls outside a window where a tutorial was going on; or racing through the narrow streets, or stealing apples from the market, or waging war. Just as she was unaware of the hidden currents of politics running below the surface of College affairs, so the Scholars, for their part, would have been unable to see the rich seething stew of alliances and enmities and feuds and treaties which was a child's life in Oxford. Children playing together: how pleasant to see! What could be more innocent and charming?

In fact, of course, Lyra and her peers were engaged in deadly warfare. First, the children (young servants, and the children of servants, and Lyra) of one college waged war on those of another. But this enmity was swept aside when the town children attacked a colleger: then all the colleges banded together and went into battle against the townies. This rivalry was hundreds of years old, and very deep and satisfying.

But even this was forgotten when the other enemies threatened. One enemy was perennial: the brick-burners' children, who lived by the Claybeds and were despised by collegers and townies alike. Last year Lyra and some townies had made a temporary truce and raided the Claybeds, pelting the brick-burners' children with lumps of heavy clay and tipping over the soggy castle they'd built, before rolling them over and over in the clinging substance they lived by until victors and vanquished alike resembled a flock of shrieking golems.

The other regular enemy was seasonal. The gyptian families, who lived in canal-boats, came and went with the spring and autumn fairs, and were always good for a fight. There was one family of gyptians in particular, who regularly returned to their mooring in that part of the city known as Jericho, with whom she'd been feuding ever since she could first throw a stone. When they were last in Oxford, she and Roger and some of the other kitchen-boys from Jordan and St Michael's College had laid an ambush for them, throwing mud at their brightly painted narrow-boat until the whole family came out to chase them away – at which point the reserve squad under Lyra raided the boat and cast it off from the bank, to float down the canal getting in the way of all the other water-traffic while Lyra's raiders searched the boat from end to end, looking for the bung. Lyra firmly believed in this bung. If they pulled it out, she assured her troop, the boat would sink at once; but they didn't find it, and had to abandon ship when the gyptians caught them up, to flee dripping and crowing with triumph through the narrow lanes of Jericho.

That was Lyra's world and her delight. She was a coarse and greedy little savage, for the most part. But she always had a dim sense that it wasn't her whole world; that part of her also belonged in the grandeur and ritual of Jordan College; and that somewhere in her life there was a connection with the high world of politics represented by Lord Asriel. All she did with that knowledge was to give herself airs and lord it over the other urchins. It had never occurred to her to find out more.

So she had passed her childhood, like a half-wild cat. The only variation in her days came on those irregular occasions when Lord Asriel visited the College. A rich and powerful uncle was all very well to boast about, but the price of boasting was having to be caught by the most agile Scholar and brought to the Housekeeper to be washed and dressed in a clean frock, following which she was escorted (with many threats) to the Senior Common Room to have tea with Lord Asriel. A group of senior Scholars would be invited as well. Lyra would slump mutinously in an armchair until the Master told her sharply to sit up, and then she'd glower at them all till even the Chaplain had to laugh.

What happened on those awkward, formal visits never varied. After the tea, the Master and the other few Scholars who'd been invited left Lyra and her uncle together, and he called her to stand in front of him and tell him what she'd learned since his last visit. And she would mutter whatever she could dredge up about geometry or Arabic or history or anbarology, and he would sit back with one ankle resting on the other knee and watch her inscrutably until her words failed.

Last year, before his expedition to the North, he'd gone on to say, "And how do you spend your time when you're not diligently studying?"

And she mumbled, "I just play. Sort of around the College. Just … play, really."

And he said, "Let me see your hands, child."

She held out her hands for inspection, and he took them and turned them over to look at her fingernails. Beside him, his dæmon lay Sphinx-like on the carpet, swishing her tail occasionally and gazing unblinkingly at Lyra.

"Dirty," said Lord Asriel, pushing her hands away. "Don't they make you wash in this place?"

"Yes," she said. "But the Chaplain's fingernails are always dirty. They're even dirtier than mine."

"He's a learned man. What's your excuse?"

"I must've got them dirty after I washed."

"Where do you play to get so dirty?"

She looked at him suspiciously. She had the feeling that being on the roof was forbidden, though no one had actually said so. "In some of the old rooms," she said finally.

"And where else?"

"In the Claybeds, sometimes."

"And?"

"Jericho and Port Meadow."

"Nowhere else?"

"No."

"You're a liar. I saw you on the roof only yesterday."

She bit her lip and said nothing. He was watching her sardonically.

"So, you play on the roof as well," he went on. "Do you ever go into the Library?"

"No. I found a rook on the Library roof, though," she went on.

"Did you? Did you catch it?"

"It had a hurt foot. I was going to kill it and roast it but Roger said we should help it get better. So we gave it scraps of food and some wine and then it got better and flew away."

"Who's Roger?"

"My friend. The Kitchen boy."

"I see. So you've been all over the roof –"

"Not all over. You can't get on to the Sheldon Building because you have to jump up from Pilgrim's Tower across a gap. There's a skylight that opens on to it, but I'm not tall enough to reach it."

"You've been all over the roof except the Sheldon Building. What about underground?"

"Underground?"

"There's as much College below ground as there is above it. I'm surprised you haven't found that out. Well, I'm going in a minute. You look healthy enough. Here."

He fished in his pocket and drew out a handful of coins, from which he gave her five gold dollars.

"Haven't they taught you to say thank you?" he said.

"Thank you," she mumbled.

"Do you obey the Master?"

"Oh, yes."

"And respect the Scholars?"

"Yes."

Lord Asriel's dæmon laughed softly. It was the first sound she'd made, and Lyra blushed.

"Go and play then," said Lord Asriel.

Lyra turned and darted to the door with relief, remembering to turn and blurt out a "Goodbye."

So Lyra's life had been, before the day when she decided to hide in the Retiring Room, and first heard about Dust.

And of course the Librarian was wrong in saying to the Master that she wouldn't have been interested. She would have listened eagerly now to anyone who could tell her about Dust. She was to hear a great deal more about it in the months to come, and eventually she would know more about Dust than anyone in the world; but in the meantime, there was all the rich life of Jordan still being lived around her.

And in any case there was something else to think about. A rumour had been filtering through the streets for some weeks: a rumour that made some people laugh and others grow silent, as some people scoff at ghosts and others fear them. For no reason that anyone could imagine, children were beginning to disappear.

It would happen like this.

East along the great highway of the River Isis, thronged with slow-moving brick-barges and asphalt-boats and corn-tankers, way down past Henley and Maidenhead to Teddington, where the tide from the German Ocean reaches, and further down still: to Mortlake, past the house of the great magician Dr Dee; past Falkeshall, where the pleasure-gardens spread out bright with fountains and banners by day, with tree-lamps and fireworks by night; past White Hall Palace, where the King holds his weekly

Council of State; past the Shot Tower, dropping its endless drizzle of molten lead into vats of murky water; further down still, to where the river, wide and filthy now, swings in a great curve to the south.

This is Limehouse, and here is the child who is going to disappear.

He is called Tony Makarios. His mother thinks he's nine years old, but she has a poor memory that the drink has rotted; he might be eight, or ten. His surname is Greek, but like his age, that is a guess on his mother's part, because he looks more Chinese than Greek, and there's Irish and Skraeling and Lascar in him from his mother's side, too. Tony's not very bright, but he has a sort of clumsy tenderness that sometimes prompts him to give his mother a rough hug and plant a sticky kiss on her cheeks. The poor woman is usually too fuddled to start such a procedure herself; but she responds warmly enough, once she realizes what's happening.

At the moment Tony is hanging about the market in Pie Street. He's hungry. It's early evening, and he won't get fed at home. He's got a shilling in his pocket that a soldier gave him for taking a message to his best girl, but Tony's not going to waste that on food, when you can pick up so much for nothing.

So he wanders through the market, between the old-clothes stalls and the fortune-paper stalls, the fruit-mongers and the fried-fish seller, with his little dæmon on his shoulder, a sparrow, watching this way and that; and when a stall-holder and her dæmon are both looking elsewhere, a brisk chirp sounds, and Tony's hand shoots out and returns to his loose shirt with an apple or a couple of nuts, and finally with a hot pie.

The stall-holder sees that, and shouts, and her cat-dæmon leaps, but Tony's sparrow is aloft and Tony himself halfway down the street already. Curses and abuse go with him, but not far. He stops running at the steps of St Catherine's Oratory, where he sits down and takes out his steaming, battered prize, leaving a trail of gravy on his shirt.

And he's being watched. A lady in a long yellow-red fox-fur coat, a beautiful young lady whose dark hair falls shining delicately under the shadow of her fur-lined hood, is standing in the doorway of the Oratory, half a dozen steps above him. It might be that a service is finishing, for light comes from the doorway behind her, an organ is playing inside, and the lady is holding a jewelled breviary.

Tony knows nothing of this. His face contentedly deep in the pie, his toes curled inwards and his bare soles together, he sits and chews and swallows while his dæmon becomes a mouse and grooms her whiskers.

The young lady's dæmon is moving out from beside the fox-fur coat. He is in the form of a monkey, but no ordinary monkey: his fur is long and silky and of the most deep and lustrous gold. With sinuous movements he inches down the steps towards the boy, and sits a step above him.

Then the mouse senses something, and becomes a sparrow again, cocking her head a fraction sideways, and hops along the stone a step or two.

The monkey watches the sparrow; the sparrow watches the monkey.

The monkey reaches out slowly. His little hand is black, his nails perfect horny claws, his movements gentle and inviting. The sparrow can't resist. She hops further, and further, and then, with a little flutter, up on to the monkey's hand.

The monkey lifts her up, and gazes closely at her before standing and swinging back to his human, taking the sparrow-dæmon with him. The lady bends her scented head to whisper.

And then Tony turns. He can't help it.

"Ratter!" he says, half in alarm, his mouth full.

The sparrow chirps. It must be safe. Tony swallows his mouthful and stares.

"Hello," says the beautiful lady. "What's your name?"

"Tony."

"Where do you live, Tony?"

"Clarice Walk."

"What's in that pie?"

"Beefsteak."

"Do you like chocolatl?"

"Yeah!"

"As it happens, I've got more chocolatl than I can drink myself. Will you come and help me drink it?"

He's lost already. He was lost the moment his slow-witted dæmon hopped on to the monkey's hand. He follows the beautiful young lady and the golden monkey down Denmark Street and along to Hangman's Wharf, and down King George's Steps to a little green door in the side of a tall warehouse. She knocks, the door is opened; they go in, the door is closed. Tony will never come out – at least, by that entrance; and he'll never see his mother again. She, poor drunken thing, will think he's run away, and when she remembers him, she'll think it was her fault, and sob her sorry heart out.

Little Tony Makarios wasn't the only child to be caught by the lady with the golden monkey. He found a dozen others in the cellar of the warehouse, boys and girls, none older than twelve or so; though since all of them had histories like his, none could be sure of their age. What Tony didn't notice, of course, was the factor that they all had in common. None of the children in that warm and steamy cellar had reached the age of puberty.

The kind lady saw him settled on a bench against the wall, and provided by a silent serving-woman with a mug of chocolatl from the saucepan on the iron stove. Tony ate the rest of his pie and drank the sweet hot liquor without taking much notice of his surroundings, and the surroundings took little notice of him: he was too small to be a threat, and too stolid to promise much satisfaction as a victim.

It was another boy who asked the obvious question.

"Hey, lady! What you got us all here for?"

He was a tough-looking wretch with dark chocolatl on his top lip and a gaunt black rat for a dæmon. The lady was standing near the door, talking to a stout man with the air of a sea-captain, and as she turned to answer, she looked so angelic in the hissing naphtha light that all the children fell silent.

"We want your help," she said. "You don't mind helping us, do you?"

No one could say a word. They all gazed, suddenly shy. They had never seen a lady like this; she was so gracious and sweet and kind that they felt they hardly deserved their good luck, and whatever she asked, they'd give it gladly so as to stay in her presence a little longer.

She told them that they were going on a voyage. They would be well fed and warmly clothed, and those who wanted to could send messages back to their families to let them know they were safe. Captain Magnusson would take them on board his ship very soon, and then when the tide was right they'd sail out to sea and set a course for the North.

Soon those few who did want to send a message to whatever home they had were sitting around the beautiful lady as she wrote a few lines at their dictation and, having let them scratch a clumsy X at the foot of the page, folded it into a scented envelope and wrote the address they told her. Tony would have liked to send something to his mother, but he had a realistic idea of her ability to read it. He plucked at the lady's fox-fur sleeve and whispered that he'd like her to tell his mum where he was going, and all, and she bent her gracious head close enough to his malodorous little body to hear, and stroked his head and promised to pass the message on.

Then the children clustered around to say goodbye. The golden monkey stroked all their dæmons, and they all touched the fox-fur for luck, or as if they were drawing some strength or hope or goodness out of the lady, and she bade them all farewell and saw them in the care of the bold captain on board a steam launch at the jetty. The sky was dark now, the river a mass of bobbing lights. The lady stood on the jetty and waved till she could see their faces no more.

Then she turned back inside, with the golden monkey nestled in her breast, and threw the little bundle of letters into the furnace before leaving the way she had come.

Children from the slums were easy enough to entice away, but eventually people noticed, and the police were stirred into reluctant action. For a while there were no more bewitchings. But a rumour had been born, and little by little it changed and grew and spread, and when after a while a few children disappeared in Norwich, and then Sheffield, and then Manchester, the people in those places who'd heard of the disappearances elsewhere added the new vanishings to the story and gave it new strength.

And so the legend grew of a mysterious group of enchanters who spirited children away. Some said their leader was a beautiful lady, others said a tall man with red eyes, while a third story told of a youth who laughed and sang to his victims so that they followed him like sheep.

As for where they took these lost children, no two stories agreed. Some said it was to Hell, under the ground, to Fairyland. Others said to a farm where the children were kept and fattened for the table. Others said that the children were kept and sold as slaves to rich Tartars… And so on.

But one thing on which everyone agreed was the name of these invisible kidnappers. They had to have a name, or not be referred to at all, and talking about them – especially if you were safe and snug at home, or in Jordan College – was delicious. And the name that seemed to settle on them, without anyone's knowing why, was the Gobblers.

"Don't stay out late, or the Gobblers'll get you!"

"My cousin in Northampton, she knows a woman whose little boy was took by the Gobblers…"

"The Gobblers've been in Stratford. They say they're coming south!"

And, inevitably:

"Let's play kids and Gobblers!"

So said Lyra to Roger the Kitchen boy from Jordan College. He would have followed her to the ends of the earth.

"How d'you play that?"

"You hide and I find you and slice you open, right, like the Gobblers do."

"You don't know what they do. They might not do that at all."

"You're afraid of 'em," she said. "I can tell."

"I en't. I don't believe in 'em, anyway."

"I do," she said decisively. "But I en't afraid either. I'd just do what my uncle done last time he came to Jordan. I seen him. He was in the Retiring Room and there was this guest who weren't polite, and my uncle just give him a hard look and the man fell dead on the spot, with all foam and froth round his mouth."

"He never," said Roger doubtfully. "They never said anything about that in the Kitchen. Anyway, you en't allowed in the Retiring Room."

"Course not. They wouldn't tell servants about a thing like that. And I *have* been in the Retiring Room, so there. Anyway, my uncle's always doing that. He done it to some Tartars when they caught him once. They tied him up and they was going to cut his guts out, but when the first man come up with the knife my uncle just looked at him, and he fell dead, so another one come up and he done the same to him, and finally there was only one left. My uncle said he'd leave him alive if he untied him, so he did, and then my uncle killed him anyway just to teach him a lesson."

Roger was less sure about that than about Gobblers, but the story was too good to waste, so they took it in turns to be Lord Asriel and the expiring Tartars, using sherbet dip for the foam.

However, that was a distraction; Lyra was still intent on playing Gobblers, and she inveigled Roger down into the wine cellars, which they entered by means of the Butler's spare set of keys. Together they crept through the great vaults where the College's Tokay and Canary, its Burgundy and brantwijn were lying under the cobwebs of ages. Ancient stone arches rose above them supported by pillars as thick as ten trees, irregular flagstones lay underfoot, and on all sides were ranged rack upon rack, tier upon tier, of bottles and barrels. It was fascinating. With Gobblers forgotten again, the two children tiptoed from end to end holding a candle in trembling fingers, peering into every dark corner, with a single question growing more urgent in Lyra's mind every moment: what did the wine taste like?

There was an easy way of answering that. Lyra – over Roger's fervent protests – picked out the oldest, twistiest, greenest bottle she could find, and, not having anything to extract the cork with, broke it off at the neck. Huddled in the furthest corner, they sipped at the heady crimson liquor, wondering when they'd become drunk, and how they'd tell when they were. Lyra didn't like the taste much, but she had to admit how grand and complicated it was. The funniest thing was watching their two dæmons, who seemed to be getting more and more muddled: falling over, giggling senselessly, and changing shape to look like gargoyles, each trying to be uglier than the other.

Finally, and almost simultaneously, the children discovered what it was like to be drunk.

"Do they *like* doing this?" gasped Roger, after vomiting copiously.

"Yes," said Lyra, in the same condition. "And so do I," she added stubbornly.

Lyra learned nothing from that episode except that playing Gobblers led to interesting places. She remembered her uncle's words in their last interview, and began to explore underground, for what was above ground was only a small fraction of the whole. Like some enormous fungus whose root-system extended over acres, Jordan (finding itself jostling for space above ground with St Michael's College on one side, Gabriel College on the other, and the University Library behind) had begun, sometime in the Middle Age, to spread below the surface. Tunnels, shafts, vaults, cellars, staircases had so hollowed out the earth below Jordan and for several hundred yards around it that there was almost as much air below ground as above; Jordan College stood on a sort of froth of stone.

And now that Lyra had the taste for exploring it, she abandoned her usual haunt, the irregular Alps of the College roofs, and plunged with Roger into this netherworld. From playing at Gobblers she had turned to hunting them, for what could be more likely than that they were lurking out of sight below the ground?

So one day she and Roger made their way into the crypt below the Oratory. This was where generations of Masters had been buried, each in his lead-lined oak coffin in niches along the stone walls. A stone tablet below each space gave their names:

Simon Le Clerc, Master 1765–1789 Cerebaton
Requiescant in pace

"What's that mean?" said Roger.

"The first part's his name, and the last bit's Roman. And there's the dates in the middle when he was Master. And the other name must be his dæmon."

They moved along the silent vault, tracing the letters of more inscriptions:

Francis Lyall, Master 1748–1765 Zohariel
Requiescant in pace

Ignatius Cole, Master 1745–1748 Musca
Requiescant in pace

On each coffin, Lyra was interested to see, a brass plaque bore a picture of a different being: this one a basilisk, this a fair woman, this a serpent, this a monkey. She realized that they were images of the dead men's dæmons. As people became adult, their dæmons lost the power to change and assumed one shape, keeping it permanently.

"These coffins've got skeletons in 'em!" whispered Roger.

"Mouldering flesh," whispered Lyra. "And worms and maggots all twisting about in their eye sockets."

"Must be ghosts down here," said Roger, shivering pleasantly.

Beyond the first crypt they found a passage lined with stone shelves. Each shelf was partitioned off into square sections, and in each section rested a skull.

Roger's dæmon, tail tucked firmly between her legs, shivered against him and gave a little quiet howl.

"Hush," he said.

Lyra couldn't see Pantalaimon, but she knew his moth-form was resting on her shoulder and probably shivering too.

She reached up and lifted the nearest skull gently out of its resting place.

"What you doing?" said Roger. "You en't supposed to touch 'em!"

She turned it over and over, taking no notice. Something suddenly fell out of the hole at the base of the skull – fell through her fingers and rang as it hit the floor, and she nearly dropped the skull in alarm.

"It's a coin!" said Roger, feeling for it. "Might be treasure!"

He held it up to the candle and they both gazed wide-eyed. It was not a coin, but a little disc of bronze with a crudely engraved inscription showing a cat.

"It's like the ones on the coffins," said Lyra. "It's his dæmon. Must be."

"Better put it back," said Roger uneasily, and Lyra upturned the skull and dropped the disc back into its immemorial resting-place before returning the skull to the shelf. Each of the other skulls, they found, had its own dæmon-coin, showing its owner's lifetime companion still close to him in death.

"Who d'you think these were when they were alive?" said Lyra. "Probably Scholars, I reckon. Only the Masters get coffins. There's probably been so many Scholars all down the centuries that there wouldn't be room to bury the whole of 'em, so they just cut their heads off and keep them. That's the most important part of 'em anyway."

They found no Gobblers, but the catacombs under the Oratory kept Lyra and Roger busy for days. Once she tried to play a trick on some of the dead Scholars, by switching around the coins in their skulls so they were with the wrong dæmons. Pantalaimon became so agitated at this that he changed into a bat and flew up and down uttering shrill cries and flapping his wings in her face, but she took no notice: it was too good a joke to waste. She paid for it later, though. In bed in her narrow room at the top of Staircase Twelve she was visited by a night-ghast, and woke up screaming at the three robed figures who stood at the bedside pointing their bony fingers before throwing back their cowls to show bleeding stumps where their heads should have been. Only when Pantalaimon became a lion and roared at them did they retreat, backing away into the substance of the wall until all that was visible was their arms, then their horny yellow-grey hands, then their twitching fingers, then nothing. First thing in the morning she hastened down to the catacombs and restored the dæmon-coins to their rightful places, and whispered "Sorry! Sorry!" to the skulls.

The catacombs were much larger than the wine-cellars, but they too had a limit. When Lyra and Roger had explored every corner of them and were sure there were no Gobblers to be found there, they turned their attention elsewhere – but not before they were spotted leaving the crypt by the Intercessor, who called them back into the Oratory.

The Intercessor was a plump, elderly man known as Father Heyst. It was his job to lead all the College services, to preach and pray and hear confessions. When Lyra was younger he had taken an interest in her spiritual welfare, only to be confounded by her sly indifference and insincere repentances. She was not spiritually promising, he had decided.

When they heard him call, Lyra and Roger turned reluctantly and walked, dragging their feet, into the great musty-smelling dimness of the Oratory. Candles flickered here and there in front of images of the saints; a faint and distant clatter came from the organ-loft, where some repairs were going on; a servant was polishing the brass lectern. Father Heyst beckoned from the vestry door.

"Where have you been?" he said to them. "I've seen you come in here two or three times now. What are you up to?"

His tone was not accusatory. He sounded as if he were genuinely interested. His dæmon flicked a lizard-tongue at them from her perch on his shoulder.

Lyra said, "We wanted to look down in the crypt."

"Whatever for?"

"The … the coffins. We wanted to see all the coffins," she said.

"But why?"

She shrugged. It was her constant response when she was pressed.

"And you," he went on, turning to Roger. Roger's dæmon anxiously wagged her terrier-tail to propitiate him. "What's your name?"

"Roger, Father."

"If you're a servant, where do you work?"

"In the Kitchen, Father."

"Should you be there now?"

"Yes, Father."

"Then be off with you."

Roger turned and ran. Lyra dragged her foot from side to side on the floor.

"As for you, Lyra," said Father Heyst, "I'm pleased to see you taking an interest in what lies in the Oratory. You are a lucky child, to have all this history around you."

"Mm," said Lyra.

"But I wonder about your choice of companions. Are you a lonely child?"

"No," she said.

"Do you... Do you miss the society of other children?"

"No."

"I don't mean Roger the Kitchen boy. I mean children such as yourself. Nobly born children. Would you like to have some companions of that sort?"

"No."

"But other girls, perhaps..."

"No."

"You see, none of us would want you to miss all the usual childhood pleasures and pastimes. I sometimes think it must be a lonely life for you here among a company of elderly Scholars, Lyra. Do you feel that?"

"No."

He tapped his thumbs together over his interlaced fingers, unable to think of anything else to ask this stubborn child.

"If there is anything troubling you," he said finally, "you know you can come and tell me about it. I hope you feel you can always do that."

"Yes," she said.

"Do you say your prayers?"

"Yes."

"Good girl. Well, run along."

With a barely concealed sigh of relief, she turned and left. Having failed to find Gobblers below ground, Lyra took to the streets again. She was at home there.

Then, almost when she'd lost interest in them, the Gobblers appeared in Oxford.

The first Lyra heard of it was when a young boy went missing from a gyptian family she knew.

It was about the time of the Horse Fair, and the canal basin was crowded with narrow boats and butty boats, with traders and travellers, and the wharves along the waterfront in Jericho were bright with gleaming harness and loud with the clop of hooves and the clamour of bargaining. Lyra always enjoyed the Horse Fair; as well as the chance of stealing a ride on a less-than-well-attended horse, there were endless opportunities for provoking warfare.

And this year she had a grand plan. Inspired by the capture of the narrow boat the year before, she intended this time to make a proper voyage before being turned out. If she and her cronies from the college kitchens could get as far as Abingdon they could play havoc with the weir…

But this year there was to be no war. As she sauntered along the edge of the boatyard in Port Meadow in the morning sun with a couple of urchins, passing a stolen cigarette from one to another and blowing out the smoke ostentatiously, she heard a cry in a voice she recognized.

"Well, what have you *done* with him, you half-arsed pillock?"

It was a mighty voice, a woman's voice, but a woman with lungs of brass and leather. Lyra looked around for her at once, because this was Ma Costa, who had clouted Lyra dizzy on two occasions but given her hot gingerbread on three, and whose family was noted for the grandeur and sumptuousness of their boat. They were princes among gyptians, and Lyra admired Ma Costa greatly, but she intended to be wary of her for some time yet, for theirs was the boat she had hijacked.

One of Lyra's brat-companions picked up a stone automatically when he heard the commotion, but Lyra said, "Put it down. She's in a temper. She could snap your backbone like a twig."

In fact, Ma Costa looked more anxious than angry. The man she was addressing, a horse-trader, was shrugging and spreading his hands.

"Well, I dunno," he was saying. "He was here one minute and gone the next. I never saw where he went…"

"He was helping you! He was holding your bloody horses for you!"

"Well, he should've stayed there, shouldn't he? Runs off in the middle of a job –"

He got no further, because Ma Costa suddenly dealt him a mighty blow on the side of the head, and followed it up with such a volley of curses and slaps that he yelled and turned to flee. The other horse-traders nearby jeered, and a flighty colt reared up in alarm.

"What's going on?" said Lyra to a gyptian child who'd been watching open-mouthed. "What's she angry about?"

"It's her kid," said the child. "It's Billy. She prob'ly reckons the Gobblers got him. They might've done, too. I ain't seen him meself since—"

"The Gobblers? Has they come to Oxford, then?"

The gyptian boy turned away to call to his friends, who were all watching Ma Costa.

"She don't know what's going on! She don't know the Gobblers is here!"

Half a dozen brats turned with expressions of derision, and Lyra threw her cigarette down, recognizing the cue for a fight. Everyone's dæmon instantly became warlike: each child was accompanied by fangs, or claws, or bristling fur, and Pantalaimon, contemptuous of the limited imaginations of these gyptian dæmons, became a dragon the size of a deer-hound.

But before they could all join battle, Ma Costa herself waded in, smacking two of the gyptians aside and confronting Lyra like a prize-fighter.

"You seen him?" she demanded of Lyra. "You seen Billy?"

"No," Lyra said. "We just got here. I en't seen Billy for months."

Ma Costa's dæmon was wheeling in the bright air above her head, a hawk, fierce yellow eyes snapping this way and that, unblinking. Lyra was frightened. No one worried about a child gone missing for a few hours, certainly not a gyptian: in the tight-knit gyptian boat-world, all children were precious and extravagantly loved, and a mother knew that if a child was out of *her* sight, it wouldn't be far from someone else's who would protect it instinctively.

But here was Ma Costa, a queen among the gyptians, in a terror for a missing child. What was going on?

Ma Costa looked half-blindly over the little group of children and turned away to stumble through the crowd on the wharf, bellowing for her child. At once the children turned back to one another, their feud abandoned in the face of her grief.

"What *is* them Gobblers?" said Simon Parslow, one of Lyra's companions.

The first gyptian boy said, "*You* know. They been stealing kids all over the country. They're pirates –"

"They en't pirates," corrected another gyptian. "They're cannaboles. That's why they call 'em Gobblers."

"They *eat* kids?" said Lyra's other crony Hugh Lovat, a Kitchen boy from St Michael's.

"No one knows," said the first gyptian. "They take 'em away and they en't never seen again."

"We all know that," said Lyra. "We been playing kids and Gobblers for months, before you were, I bet. But I bet no one's seen 'em."

"They have," said one boy.

"Who, then?" persisted Lyra. "Have *you* seen 'em? How d'you know it en't just one person?"

"Charlie seen 'em in Banbury," said a gyptian girl. "They

come and talked to this lady while another man took her little boy out the garden."

"Yeah," piped up Charlie, a gyptian boy. "I seen 'em do it!"

"What did they look like?" said Lyra.

"Well … I never properly saw 'em," Charlie said. "I saw their truck, though," he added. "They come in a white truck. They put the little boy in the truck and drove off quick."

"But why do they call 'em Gobblers?" Lyra asked.

"'Cause they eat 'em," said the first gyptian boy. "Someone told us in Northampton. They been up there and all. This girl in Northampton, her brother was took, and she said the men as took him told her they was going to eat him. Everyone knows that. They gobble 'em up."

A gyptian girl standing nearby began to cry loudly.

"That's Billy's cousin," said Charlie.

Lyra said, "Who saw Billy last?"

"Me," said half a dozen voices. "I seen him holding Johnny Fiorelli's old horse – I seen him by the toffee-apple seller – I seen him swinging on the crane –"

When Lyra had sorted it out, she gathered that Billy had been seen for certain not less than two hours previously.

"So," she said, "some time in the last two hours there must've been Gobblers here…"

They all looked around, shivering in spite of the warm sun, the crowded wharf, the familiar smells of tar and horses and smoking-leaf. The trouble was that because no one knew what these Gobblers looked like, anyone might be a Gobbler, as Lyra pointed out to the appalled gang, who were now all under her sway, collegers and gyptians alike.

"They're *bound* to look like ordinary people, else they'd be seen at once," she explained. "If they only came at night, they could look like anything. But if they come in the daylight they got

57

to look ordinary. So any of these people might be Gobblers…"

"They en't," said a gyptian uncertainly. "I know 'em all."

"All right, not *these*, but anyone else," said Lyra. "Let's go and look for 'em! And their white truck!"

And that precipitated a swarm. Other searchers soon joined the first ones, and before long, thirty or more gyptian children were racing from end to end of the wharves, running in and out of stables, scrambling over the cranes and derricks in the boatyard, leaping over the fence into the wide meadow, swinging fifteen at a time on the old swing bridge over the green water, and running full pelt through the narrow streets of Jericho, between the little brick terraced houses and into the great square-towered oratory of St Barnabas the Chymist. Half of them didn't know what they were looking for, and thought it was just a lark, but those closest to Lyra felt a real fear and apprehension every time they glimpsed a solitary figure down an alley or in the dimness of the Oratory: was it a Gobbler?

But of course they weren't. Eventually, with no success, and with the shadow of Billy's real disappearance hanging over them all, the fun faded away. As Lyra and the two college boys left Jericho when supper-time neared, they saw the gyptians gathering on the wharf next to where the Costas' boat was moored. Some of the women were crying loudly, and the men were standing in angry groups, with all their dæmons agitated and rising in nervous flight or snarling at shadows.

"I bet them Gobblers wouldn't dare come in here," said Lyra to Simon Parslow, as the two of them stepped over the threshold into the great lodge of Jordan.

"No," he said uncertainly. "But I know there's a kid missing from the Market."

"Who?" Lyra said. She knew most of the Market children, but she hadn't heard of this.

"Jessie Reynolds, out the saddler's. She weren't there at shutting-up time yesterday, and she'd only gone for a bit of fish for her dad's tea. She never come back and no one'd seen her. They searched all through the Market and everywhere."

"I never heard about that!" said Lyra, indignant. She considered it a deplorable lapse on the part of her subjects not to tell her everything and at once.

"Well, it was only yesterday. She might've turned up now."

"I'm going to ask," said Lyra, and turned to leave the Lodge.

But she hadn't got out of the gate before the Porter called her.

"Here, Lyra! You're not to go out again this evening. Master's orders."

"Why not?"

"I told you, Master's orders. He says if you come in, you stay in."

"You catch me," she said, and darted out before the old man could leave his doorway.

She ran across the narrow street and down into the alley where the vans unloaded goods for the Covered Market. This being shutting-up time, there were few vans there now, but a knot of youths stood smoking and talking by the central gate opposite the high stone wall of St Michael's College. Lyra knew one of them, a sixteen-year-old she admired because he could spit further than anyone else she'd ever heard of, and she went and waited humbly for him to notice her.

"Yeah? What do you want?" he said finally.

"Is Jessie Reynolds disappeared?"

"Yeah. Why?"

"'Cause a gyptian kid disappeared today and all."

"They're always disappearing, gyptians. After every Horse Fair they disappear."

"So do horses," said one of his friends.

"This is different," said Lyra. "This is a kid. We was looking for him all afternoon and the other kids said the Gobblers got him."

"The what?"

"The Gobblers," she said. "En't you heard of the Gobblers?"

It was news to the other boys as well, and apart from a few coarse comments they listened closely to what she told them.

"Gobblers," said Lyra's acquaintance, whose name was Dick. "It's stupid. These gyptians, they pick up all kinds of stupid ideas."

"They said there was Gobblers in Banbury a couple of weeks ago," Lyra insisted, "and there was five kids taken. They probably come to Oxford now to get kids from us. It must've been them what got Jessie."

"There was a kid lost over Cowley way," said one of the other boys. "I remember now. My auntie, she was there yesterday, 'cause she sells fish and chips out a van, and she heard about it... Some little boy, that's it... I dunno about the Gobblers, though. They en't real, Gobblers. Just a story."

"They are!" Lyra said. "The gyptians seen 'em. They reckon they eat the kids they catch, and..."

She stopped in mid-sentence, because something had suddenly come into her mind. During that strange evening she'd spent hidden in the Retiring Room, Lord Asriel had shown a lantern slide of a man holding up a wand with streams of light pouring into it; and there'd been a small figure beside him, with less light around it; and he'd said it was a child; and someone had asked if it was a severed child, and her uncle had said no, that was the point. Lyra remembered that severed meant cut.

And then something else hit her heart: where was Roger?

She hadn't seen him since the morning...

Suddenly she felt afraid. Pantalaimon, as a miniature lion, sprang into her arms and growled. She said goodbye to the youths by the gate and walked quietly back into Turl Street, and then ran full pelt for Jordan Lodge, tumbling in through the door a second before the now cheetah-shaped dæmon.

The Porter was sanctimonious.

"I had to ring the Master and tell him," he said. "He en't pleased at all. I wouldn't be in your shoes, not for money I wouldn't."

"Where's Roger?" she demanded.

"I en't seen him. He'll be for it, too. Ooh, when Mr Cawston catches him –"

Lyra ran to the Kitchen and thrust her way into the hot, clangorous, steaming bustle.

"Where's Roger?" she shouted.

"Clear off, Lyra! We're busy here!"

"But where is he? Has he turned up or not?"

No one seemed interested.

"But where is he? You *must've* heard!" Lyra shouted at the chef, who boxed her ears and sent her storming away.

Bernie the pastrycook tried to calm her down, but she wouldn't be consoled.

"They got him! Them bloody Gobblers, they oughter catch 'em and bloody kill 'em! I hate 'em! You don't care about Roger –"

"Lyra, we all care about Roger –"

"You don't, else you'd all stop work and go and look for him right now! I hate you!"

"There could be a dozen reasons why Roger en't turned up. Listen to sense. We got dinner to prepare and serve in less than an hour; the Master's got guests in the Lodging, and he'll be eating over there, and that means Chef'll have to attend to getting the food there quick so it don't go cold; and what with one thing and another, Lyra, life's got to go on. I'm sure Roger'll turn up…"

Lyra turned and ran out of the Kitchen, knocking over a stack of silver dish-covers and ignoring the roar of anger that arose. She sped down the steps and across the quadrangle, between the Chapel and Palmer's Tower and into the Yaxley Quad, where the oldest buildings of the College stood.

Pantalaimon scampered before her like a miniature cheetah, flowing up the stairs to the very top, where Lyra's bedroom was. Lyra barged open the door, dragged her rickety chair to the window, flung wide the casement and scrambled out. There was a lead-lined stone gutter a foot wide just below the window, and once she was standing in that, she turned and clambered up over the rough tiles until she stood on the topmost ridge of the roof. There she opened her mouth and screamed. Pantalaimon, who always became a bird once on the roof, flew round and round shrieking rook-shrieks with her.

The evening sky was awash with peach, apricot, cream: tender little ice-cream clouds in a wide orange sky. The spires and towers of Oxford stood around them, level but no higher; the green woods of Château-Vert and White Ham rose on either side to the east and the west. Rooks were cawing somewhere, and bells were ringing, and from the Oxpens the steady beat of a gas engine announced the ascent of the evening Royal Mail zeppelin for London. Lyra watched it climb away beyond the spire of St Michael's Chapel, as big at first as the tip of her little finger when she held it at arm's length, and then steadily smaller until it was a dot in the pearly sky.

She turned and looked down into the shadowed quadrangle, where the black-gowned figures of the Scholars were already beginning to drift in ones and twos towards the Buttery, their dæmons strutting or fluttering alongside or perching calmly on their shoulders. The lights were going on in the Hall; she could see the stained-glass windows gradually beginning to glow as a servant moved up the tables lighting the naphtha lamps. The Steward's bell began to toll, announcing half an hour before dinner.

This was her world. She wanted it to stay the same for ever and ever, but it was changing around her, for someone out there was stealing children. She sat on the roof-ridge, chin in hands.

"We better rescue him, Pantalaimon," she said.

He answered in his rook-voice from the chimney.

"It'll be dangerous," he said.

"Course! I know that."

"Remember what they said in the Retiring Room."

"What?"

"Something about a child up in the Arctic. The one that wasn't attracting the Dust."

"They said it was an entire child... What about it?"

"That might be what they're going to do to Roger and the gyptians and the other kids."

"What?"

"Well, what does *entire* mean?"

"Dunno. They cut 'em in half, probably. I reckon they make slaves out of 'em. That'd be more use. They probably got mines up there. Uranium mines for atomcraft. I bet that's what it is. And if they sent grown-ups down the mine they'd be dead, so they use kids instead because they cost less. That's what they've done with him."

"I think –"

But what Pantalaimon thought had to wait, because someone began to shout from below.

"Lyra! Lyra! You come in this instant!"

There was a banging on the window-frame. Lyra knew the

voice and the impatience: it was Mrs Lonsdale the Housekeeper. There was no hiding from her.

Tight-faced, Lyra slid down the roof and into the gutter, and then climbed in through the window again. Mrs Lonsdale was running some water into the little chipped basin, to the accompaniment of a great groaning and hammering from the pipes.

"The number of times you been told about going out there… Look at you! Just look at your skirt – it's filthy! Take it off at once and wash yourself while I look for something decent that en't torn. Why you can't keep yourself clean and tidy…"

Lyra was too sulky even to ask why she was having to wash and dress, and no grown-up ever gave reasons of their own accord. She dragged the dress over her head and dropped it on the narrow bed, and began to wash desultorily while Pantalaimon, a canary now, hopped closer and closer to Mrs Lonsdale's dæmon, a stolid retriever, trying in vain to annoy him.

"Look at the state of this wardrobe! You en't hung nothing up for weeks! Look at the creases in this –"

Look at this, look at that … Lyra didn't want to look. She shut her eyes as she rubbed at her face with the thin towel.

"You'll just have to wear it as it is. There en't time to take an iron to it. God bless me, girl, your *knees* – look at the state of them…"

"Don't want to look at nothing," Lyra muttered.

Mrs Lonsdale smacked her leg. "Wash," she said ferociously. "You get all that dirt off."

"Why?" Lyra said at last. "I never wash my knees usually. No one's going to look at my knees. What've I got to do all this for? You don't care about Roger neither, any more than Chef does. I'm the only one that –"

Another smack, on the other leg.

"None of that nonsense. I'm a Parslow, same as Roger's father. He's my second cousin. I bet you didn't know that, 'cause I bet you never asked, Miss Lyra. I bet it never occurred to you. Don't you chide me with not caring about the boy. God knows, I even care about you, and you give me little enough reason and no thanks."

She seized the flannel and rubbed Lyra's knees so hard she left the skin bright pink and sore, but clean.

"The reason for this is you're going to have dinner with the Master and his guests. I hope to God you behave. Speak when you're spoken to, be quiet and polite, smile nicely and don't you ever say *Dunno* when someone asks you a question."

She dragged the best dress on to Lyra's skinny frame, tugged it straight, fished a bit of red ribbon out of the tangle in a drawer, and brushed Lyra's hair with a coarse brush.

"If they'd let me know earlier I could've given your hair a proper wash. Well, that's too bad. As long as they don't look too close… There. Now stand up straight. Where's those best patent-leather shoes?"

Five minutes later Lyra was knocking on the door of the Master's Lodging, the grand and slightly gloomy house that opened into the Yaxley Quadrangle and backed on to the Library Garden. Pantalaimon, an ermine now for politeness, rubbed himself against her leg. The door was opened by the Master's manservant Cousins, an old enemy of Lyra's; but both knew that this was a state of truce.

"Mrs Lonsdale said I was to come," said Lyra.

"Yes," said Cousins, stepping aside. "The Master's in the Drawing Room."

He showed her into the large room that overlooked the Library Garden. The last of the sun shone into it, through the gap between the Library and Palmer's Tower, and lit up the heavy pictures and the glum silver the Master collected. It also lit up the guests, and Lyra realized why they weren't going to dine in Hall: three of the guests were women.

"Ah, Lyra," said the Master. "I'm so glad you could come. Cousins, could you find some sort of soft drink? Dame Hannah, I don't think you've met Lyra ... Lord Asriel's niece, you know."

Dame Hannah Relf was the Head of one of the women's colleges, an elderly grey-haired lady whose dæmon was a marmoset. Lyra shook hands as politely as she could, and was then introduced to the other guests, who were, like Dame Hannah, scholars from other Colleges and quite uninteresting. Then the Master came to the final guest.

"Mrs Coulter," he said, "this is our Lyra. Lyra, come and say hello to Mrs Coulter."

"Hello, Lyra," said Mrs Coulter.

She was beautiful and young. Her sleek black hair framed her cheeks, and her dæmon was a golden monkey.

4

The Alethiometer

 "I hope you'll sit next to me at dinner," said Mrs Coulter, making room for Lyra on the sofa. "I'm not used to the grandeur of a Master's Lodging. You'll have to show me which knife and fork to use."

"Are you a female Scholar?" said Lyra. She regarded female Scholars with a proper Jordan disdain: there *were* such people but, poor things, they could never be taken more seriously than animals dressed up and acting a play. Mrs Coulter, on the other hand, was not like any female Scholar Lyra had seen, and certainly not like the two serious elderly ladies who were the other female guests. Lyra had asked the question expecting the answer no, in fact, for Mrs Coulter had such an air of glamour that Lyra was entranced. She could hardly take her eyes off her.

"Not really," Mrs Coulter said. "I'm a member of Dame Hannah's college, but most of my work takes place outside Oxford… Tell me about yourself, Lyra. Have you always lived at Jordan College?"

Within five minutes Lyra had told her everything about her half-wild life: her favourite routes over the roof-tops, the battle of the Claybeds, the time she and Roger had caught and roasted a rook, her intention to capture a narrow-boat from the gyptians and sail it to Abingdon, and so on. She even (looking around and lowering her voice) told her about the trick she and Roger had played on the skulls in the crypt.

"And these ghosts came, right, they came to my bedroom without their heads! They couldn't talk except for making sort of gurgling noises, but I knew what they wanted all right. So I went down next day and put their coins back. They'd probably have killed me else."

"You're not afraid of danger, then?" said Mrs Coulter admiringly. They were at dinner by this time, and as Mrs Coulter had hoped, sitting next to each other. Lyra ignored completely the Librarian on her other side and spent the whole meal talking to Mrs Coulter.

When the ladies withdrew for coffee, Dame Hannah said, "Tell me, Lyra – are they going to send you to school?"

Lyra looked blank. "I dun – I don't know," she said. "Probably not," she added for safety. "I wouldn't want to put them to any trouble," she went on piously. "Or expense. It's probably better if I just go on living at Jordan and getting educated by the Scholars here when they've got a bit of spare time. Being as they're here already, they're probably free."

"And does your uncle Lord Asriel have any plans for you?" said the other lady, who was a Scholar at the other women's college.

"Yes," said Lyra. "I expect so. Not school, though. He's going to take me to the North next time he goes."

"I remember him telling me," said Mrs Coulter.

Lyra blinked. The two female Scholars sat up very slightly, though their dæmons, either well-behaved or torpid, did no more than flick their eyes at each other.

"I met him at the Royal Arctic Institute," Mrs Coulter went on. "As a matter of fact it's partly because of that meeting that I'm here today."

"Are you an explorer too?" said Lyra.

"In a kind of way. I've been to the North several times. Last year I spent three months in Greenland making observations of the Aurora."

That was it; nothing and no one else existed now for Lyra. She gazed at Mrs Coulter with awe, and listened rapt and silent to her tales of igloo-building, of seal-hunting, of negotiating with the Lapland witches. The two female Scholars had nothing so exciting to tell, and sat in silence until the men came in.

Later, when the guests were preparing to leave, the Master said, "Stay behind, Lyra. I'd like to talk to you for a minute or two. Go to my study, child; sit down there and wait for me."

Puzzled, tired, exhilarated, Lyra did as he told her. Cousins the manservant showed her in, and pointedly left the door open so that he could see what she was up to from the hall, where he was helping people on with their coats. Lyra watched for Mrs Coulter, but she didn't see her, and then the Master came into the study and shut the door.

He sat down heavily in the armchair by the fireplace. His dæmon flapped up to the chair-back and sat by his head, her old hooded eyes on Lyra. The lamp hissed gently as the Master said:

"So, Lyra. You've been talking to Mrs Coulter. Did you enjoy hearing what she said?"

"Yes!"

"She is a remarkable lady."

"She's wonderful. She's the most wonderful person I've ever met."

The Master sighed. In his black suit and black tie he looked as much like his dæmon as anyone could, and suddenly Lyra thought that one day, quite soon, he would be buried in the crypt under the Oratory, and an artist would engrave a picture of his dæmon on the brass plate for his coffin, and her name would share the space with his.

"I should have made time before now for a talk with you, Lyra," he said after a few moments. "I was intending to do so in any case, but it seems that time is further on than I thought. You have been safe here in Jordan, my dear. I think you've been happy. You haven't found it easy to obey us, but we are very fond of you, and you've never been a bad child. There's a lot of goodness and sweetness in your nature, and a lot of determination. You're going to need all of that. Things are going on in the wide world I would have liked to protect you from – by keeping you here in Jordan, I mean – but that's no longer possible."

She merely stared. Were they going to send her away?

"You knew that sometime you'd have to go to school," the Master went on. "We have taught you some things here, but not well or systematically. Our knowledge is of a different kind. You need to know things that elderly men are not able to teach you, especially at the age you are now. You must have been aware of that. You're not a servant's child either; we couldn't put you out to be fostered by a town family. They might have cared for you in some ways, but your needs are different. You see, what I'm saying to you, Lyra, is that the part of your life that belongs to Jordan College is coming to an end."

"No," she said, "no, I don't want to leave Jordan. I like it here. I want to stay here for ever."

"When you're young, you do think that things last for ever. Unfortunately, they don't. Lyra, it won't be long – a couple of years at most – before you will be a young woman, and not a child any more. A young lady. And believe me, you'll find Jordan College a far from easy place to live in then."

"But it's my home!"

"It has been your home. But now you need something else."

"Not school. I'm not going to school."

"You need female company. Female guidance."

The word *female* only suggested female Scholars to Lyra, and she involuntarily made a face. To be exiled from the grandeur of Jordan, the splendour and fame of its scholarship, to a dingy brick-built boarding-house of a college at the northern end of Oxford, with dowdy female Scholars who smelt of cabbage and mothballs like those two at dinner!

The Master saw her expression, and saw Pantalaimon's polecat-eyes flash red.

He said, "But suppose it were Mrs Coulter?"

Instantly Pantalaimon's fur changed from coarse brown to downy white. Lyra's eyes widened.

"Really?"

"She is by way of being acquainted with Lord Asriel. Your uncle, of course, is very concerned with your welfare, and when Mrs Coulter heard about you, she offered at once to help. There is no Mr Coulter, by the way; she is a widow; her husband died very sadly in an accident some years ago; so you might bear that in mind before you ask."

Lyra nodded eagerly, and said, "And she's really going to … look after me?"

"Would you like that?"

"Yes!"

She could hardly sit still. The Master smiled. He smiled so rarely that he was out of practice, and anyone watching (Lyra wasn't in a state to notice) would have said it was a grimace of sadness.

"Well, we had better ask her in to talk about it," he said.

He left the room, and when he came back a minute later with Mrs Coulter, Lyra was on her feet, too excited to sit. Mrs

71

Coulter smiled, and her dæmon bared his white teeth in a grin of imp-like pleasure. As she passed her on the way to the armchair, Mrs Coulter touched Lyra's hair briefly, and Lyra felt a current of warmth flow into her, and blushed.

When the Master had poured some brantwijn for her, Mrs Coulter said, "So, Lyra, I'm to have an assistant, am I?"

"Yes," said Lyra simply. She would have said yes to anything.

"There's a lot of work I need help with."

"I can work!"

"And we might have to travel."

"I don't mind. I'd go anywhere."

"But it might be dangerous. We might have to go to the North."

Lyra was speechless. Then she found her voice: "Soon?"

Mrs Coulter laughed, and said, "Possibly. But you know you'll have to work very hard. You'll have to learn mathematics, and navigation, and celestial geography."

"Will *you* teach me?"

"Yes. And you'll have to help me by making notes and putting my papers in order and doing various pieces of basic calculation, and so on. And because we'll be visiting some important people, we'll have to find you some pretty clothes. There's a lot to learn, Lyra."

"I don't mind. I want to learn it all."

"I'm sure you will. When you come back to Jordan College you'll be a famous traveller. Now we're going to leave very early in the morning, by the dawn zeppelin, so you'd better run along and go straight to bed. I'll see you at breakfast. Good night!"

"Good night," said Lyra and, remembering the few manners she had, turned at the door and said, "Good night, Master."

He nodded. "Sleep well," he said.

"And thanks," Lyra added to Mrs Coulter.

* * *

She did sleep, finally, though Pantalaimon wouldn't settle until she snapped at him, when he became a hedgehog out of pique. It was still dark when someone shook her awake.

"Lyra – hush – don't start – wake up, child."

It was Mrs Lonsdale. She was holding a candle, and she bent over and spoke quietly, holding Lyra still with her free hand.

"Listen. The Master wants to see you before you join Mrs Coulter for breakfast. Get up quickly and run across to the Lodging now. Go into the garden and tap at the French window of the study. You understand?"

Fully awake and on fire with puzzlement, Lyra nodded and slipped her bare feet into the shoes Mrs Lonsdale put down for her.

"Never mind washing – that'll do later. Go straight down and come straight back. I'll start your packing and have something for you to wear. Hurry now."

The dark quadrangle was still full of the chill night air. Overhead the last stars were still visible, but the light from the east was gradually soaking into the sky above the Hall. Lyra ran into the Library Garden, and stood for a moment in the immense hush, looking up at the stone pinnacles of the Chapel, the pearl-green cupola of the Sheldon Building, the white-painted lantern of the Library. Now she was going to leave these sights, she wondered how much she'd miss them.

Something stirred in the study window and a glow of light shone out for a moment. She remembered what she had to do and tapped on the glass door. It opened almost at once.

"Good girl. Come in quickly. We haven't got long," said the Master, and drew the curtain back across the door as soon as she had entered. He was fully dressed in his usual black.

"Aren't I going after all?" Lyra asked.

"Yes; I can't prevent it," said the Master, and Lyra didn't notice at the time what an odd thing that was to say. "Lyra, I'm going to give you something, and you must promise to keep it private. Will you swear to that?"

"Yes," Lyra said.

He crossed to the desk and took from a drawer a small package wrapped in black velvet. When he unfolded the cloth, Lyra saw something like a large watch or a small clock: a thick disc of brass and crystal. It might have been a compass or something of the sort.

"What is it?" she said.

"It's an alethiometer. It's one of only six that were ever made. Lyra, I urge you again: keep it private. It would be better if Mrs Coulter didn't know about it. Your uncle –"

"But what does it do?"

"It tells you the truth. As for how to read it, you'll have to learn by yourself. Now go – it's getting lighter – hurry back to your room before anyone sees you."

He folded the velvet over the instrument and thrust it into her hands. It was surprisingly heavy. Then he put his own hands on either side of her head and held her gently for a moment.

She tried to look up at him, and said, "What were you going to say about Uncle Asriel?"

"Your uncle presented it to Jordan College some years ago. He might –"

Before he could finish, there came a soft urgent knock on the door. She could feel his hands give an involuntary tremor.

"Quick now, child," he said quietly. "The powers of this world are very strong. Men and women are moved by tides much fiercer than you can imagine, and they sweep us all up into the current. Go well, Lyra; bless you, child; bless you. Keep your own counsel."

"Thank you, Master," she said dutifully.

Clutching the bundle to her breast, she left the study by the garden door, looking back briefly once to see the Master's dæmon watching her from the windowsill. The sky was lighter already; there was a faint fresh stir in the air.

"What's that you've got?" said Mrs Lonsdale, closing the battered little suitcase with a snap.

"The Master gave it me. Can't it go in the suitcase?"

"Too late. I'm not opening it now. It'll have to go in your coat pocket, whatever it is. Hurry on down to the Buttery; don't keep them waiting…"

It was only after she'd said goodbye to the few servants who were up, and to Mrs Lonsdale, that she remembered Roger; and then she felt guilty for not having thought of him once since meeting Mrs Coulter. How quickly it had all happened!

And now she was on her way to London: sitting next to the window in a zeppelin, no less, with Pantalaimon's sharp little ermine-paws digging into her thigh while his front paws rested against the glass he gazed through. On Lyra's other side Mrs Coulter sat working through some papers, but she soon put them away and talked. Such brilliant talk! Lyra was intoxicated; not about the North this time, but about London, and the restaurants and ballrooms, the soirées at Embassies or Ministries, the intrigues between White Hall and Westminster. Lyra was almost more fascinated by this than by the changing landscape below the airship. What Mrs Coulter was saying seemed to be accompanied by a scent of grown-upness, something disturbing but enticing at the same time: it was the smell of glamour.

The landing in Falkeshall Gardens, the boat ride across the wide brown river, the grand mansion-block on the Embankment where a stout commissionaire (a sort of porter with medals) saluted Mrs Coulter and winked at Lyra, who sized him up expressionlessly…

And then the flat…

Lyra could only gasp.

She had seen a great deal of beauty in her short life, but it was Jordan College beauty, Oxford beauty – grand and stony and masculine. In Jordan College, much was magnificent, but nothing was pretty. In Mrs Coulter's flat, everything was pretty. It was full of light, for the wide windows faced south, and the walls were covered in a delicate gold-and-white striped wallpaper. Charming pictures in gilt frames, an antique looking-glass, fanciful sconces bearing anbaric lamps with frilled shades; and frills on the cushions too, and flowery valances over the curtain-rail, and a soft green leaf-pattern carpet underfoot; and every surface was covered, it seemed to Lyra's innocent eye, with pretty little china boxes and shepherdesses and harlequins of porcelain.

Mrs Coulter smiled at her admiration.

"Yes, Lyra," she said, "there's such a lot to show you! Take your coat off and I'll take you to the bathroom. You can have a wash, and then we'll have some lunch and go shopping…"

The bathroom was another wonder. Lyra was used to washing with hard yellow soap in a chipped basin, where the water that struggled out of the taps was warm at best, and often flecked with rust. But here the water was hot, the soap rose-pink and fragrant, the towels thick and cloudy-soft. And around the edge of the tinted mirror there were little pink lights, so that when Lyra looked into it she saw a softly illuminated figure quite unlike the Lyra she knew.

Pantalaimon, who was imitating the form of Mrs Coulter's dæmon, crouched on the edge of the basin making faces at her. She pushed him into the soapy water and suddenly remembered the alethiometer in her coat pocket. She'd left the coat on a chair in the other room. She'd promised the Master to keep it secret from Mrs Coulter…

Oh, this *was* confusing. Mrs Coulter was so kind and wise, whereas Lyra had actually seen the Master trying to poison Uncle Asriel. Which of them did she owe most obedience to?

She rubbed herself dry hastily and hurried back to the sitting room, where her coat still lay untouched, of course.

"Ready?" said Mrs Coulter. "I thought we'd go to the Royal Arctic Institute for lunch. I'm one of the very few female members, so I might as well use the privileges I have."

Twenty minutes' walk took them to a grand stone-fronted building where they sat in a wide dining-room with snowy cloths and bright silver on the tables, and ate calves' liver and bacon.

"Calves' liver is all right," Mrs Coulter told her, "and so is seal liver, but if you're stuck for food in the Arctic, you mustn't eat bear liver. That's full of a poison that'll kill you in minutes."

As they ate, Mrs Coulter pointed out some of the members at the other tables.

"D'you see the elderly gentleman with the red tie? That's Colonel Carborn. He made the first balloon flight over the North Pole. And the tall man by the window who's just got up is Dr Broken Arrow."

"Is he a Skraeling?"

"Yes. He was the man who mapped the ocean currents in the Great Northern Ocean…"

Lyra looked at them all, these great men, with curiosity and awe. They were scholars, no doubt about that, but they were explorers too. Dr Broken Arrow would know about bear livers; she doubted whether the Librarian of Jordan College would.

After lunch Mrs Coulter showed her some of the precious Arctic relics in the Institute Library – the harpoon with which the great whale Grimssdur had been killed; the stone carved with an inscription in an unknown language which was found in the hand of the explorer Lord Rukh, frozen to death in his lonely tent; a fire-striker used by Captain Hudson on his famous voyage to Van Tieren's Land. She told the story of each one, and Lyra felt her heart stir with admiration of these great, brave, distant heroes.

And then they went shopping. Everything on this extraordinary day was a new experience for Lyra, but shopping was the most dizzying. To go into a vast building full of beautiful clothes, where people let you try them on, where you looked at yourself in mirrors… And the clothes were so *pretty*… Lyra's clothes had come to her through Mrs Lonsdale, and a lot of them had been handed down and much mended. She had seldom had anything new, and when she had, it had been picked for wear and not for looks; and she had never chosen anything for herself. And now to find Mrs Coulter suggesting this, and praising that, and paying for it all, and more…

By the time they'd finished, Lyra was flushed and bright-eyed with tiredness. Mrs Coulter ordered most of the clothes packed up and delivered, and took one or two things with her when she and Lyra walked back to the flat.

Then a bath, with thick scented foam. Mrs Coulter came into the bathroom to wash Lyra's hair, and she didn't rub and scrape like Mrs Lonsdale either. She was gentle. Pantalaimon watched with powerful curiosity until Mrs Coulter looked at him, and he knew what she meant and turned away, averting his eyes modestly from these feminine mysteries as the golden monkey was doing. He had never had to look away from Lyra before.

Then, after the bath, a warm drink with milk and herbs; and a new flannel nightdress with printed flowers and a scalloped hem, and sheepskin slippers dyed soft blue; and then bed.

So soft, this bed! So gentle, the anbaric light on the bedside table! And the bedroom so cosy with little cupboards and a dressing-table and a chest of drawers where her new clothes would go, and a carpet from one wall to the other, and pretty curtains covered in stars and moons and planets! Lyra lay stiffly, too tired to sleep, too enchanted to question anything.

When Mrs Coulter had wished her a soft good night and gone out, Pantalaimon plucked at her hair. She brushed him away, but he whispered, "Where's the thing?"

She knew at once what he meant. Her old shabby overcoat hung in the wardrobe; a few seconds later, she was back in bed, sitting up cross-legged in the lamplight, with Pantalaimon watching closely as she unfolded the black velvet and looked at what it was the Master had given her.

"What did he call it?" she whispered.

"An alethiometer."

There was no point in asking what that meant. It lay heavily in her hands, the crystal face gleaming, the brass body exquisitely machined. It was very like a clock, or a compass, for there were hands pointing to places around the dial, but instead of the hours or the points of the compass there were several little pictures, each of them painted with extraordinary precision, as if on ivory with the finest and slenderest sable brush. She turned the dial around to look at them all. There was an anchor; an hourglass surmounted by a skull; a bull, a beehive... Thirty-six altogether, and she couldn't even guess what they meant.

"There's a wheel, look," said Pantalaimon. "See if you can wind it up."

There were three little knurled winding-wheels, in fact, and each of them turned one of the three shorter hands, which moved around the dial in a series of smooth satisfying clicks. You could arrange them to point at any of the pictures, and once they had clicked into position, pointing exactly at the centre of each one, they would not move.

The fourth hand was longer and more slender, and seemed to be made of a duller metal than the other three. Lyra couldn't control its movement at all; it swung where it wanted to, like a compass-needle, except that it didn't settle.

"Meter means measure," said Pantalaimon. "Like thermometer. The Chaplain told us that."

"Yes, but that's the easy bit," she whispered back. "What d'you think it's *for*?"

Neither of them could guess. Lyra spent a long time turning the hands to point at one symbol or another (angel, helmet, dolphin; globe, lute, compasses; candle, thunderbolt, horse) and watching the long needle swing on its never-ceasing errant way, and although she understood nothing, she was intrigued and delighted by the complexity and the detail. Pantalaimon became a mouse to get closer to it, and rested his tiny paws on the edge, his button eyes bright black with curiosity as he watched the needle swing.

"What do you think the Master meant about Uncle Asriel?" she said.

"Perhaps we've got to keep it safe and give it to him."

"But the Master was going to poison him! Perhaps it's the opposite. Perhaps he was going to say, don't give it to him."

"No," Pantalaimon said, "it was *her* we had to keep it safe from –"

There was a soft knock on the door.

Mrs Coulter said, "Lyra, I should put the light out if I were you. You're tired, and we'll be busy tomorrow."

Lyra had thrust the alethiometer swiftly under the blankets.

"All right, Mrs Coulter," she said.

"Good night now."

"Good night."

She snuggled down and switched off the light. Before she fell asleep, she tucked the alethiometer under the pillow, just in case.

5

The Cocktail Party

In the days that followed, Lyra went everywhere with Mrs Coulter, almost as if she were a dæmon herself. Mrs Coulter knew a great many people, and they met in all kinds of different places. In the morning there might be a meeting of geographers at the Royal Arctic Institute, and Lyra would sit by and listen; and then Mrs Coulter might meet a politician or a cleric for lunch in a smart restaurant, and they would be very taken with Lyra and order special dishes for her, and she would learn how to eat asparagus or what sweetbreads tasted like. And then in the afternoon there might be more shopping, for Mrs Coulter was preparing her expedition, and there were furs and oilskins and waterproof boots to buy, as well as sleeping-bags and knives and drawing instruments that delighted Lyra's heart. After that they might go to tea and meet some ladies, as well-dressed as Mrs Coulter if not so beautiful or accomplished: women so unlike female scholars or gyptian boat-mothers or college servants as almost to be a new sex altogether, one with dangerous powers and qualities such as elegance, charm, and grace. Lyra would be dressed up prettily for these occasions, and the ladies would pamper her and include her in their graceful delicate talk, which was all about people: this artist, or that politician, or those lovers.

And when the evening came, Mrs Coulter might take Lyra to the theatre, and again there would be lots of glamorous people to talk to and be admired by, for it seemed that Mrs Coulter knew everyone important in London.

In the intervals between all these other activities Mrs Coulter would teach her the rudiments of geography and mathematics. Lyra's knowledge had great gaps in it, like a map of the world largely eaten by mice, for at Jordan they had taught her in a piecemeal and disconnected way: a Junior Scholar would be detailed to catch her and instruct her in such-and-such, and the lessons would continue for a sullen week or so until she "forgot" to turn up, to the Scholar's relief. Or else a Scholar would forget what he was supposed to teach her, and drill her at great length about the subject of his current research, whatever that happened to be. It was no wonder her knowledge was patchy. She knew about atoms and elementary particles, and anbaromagnetic charges and the four fundamental forces and other bits and pieces of experimental theology, but nothing about the solar system. In fact, when Mrs Coulter realized this and explained how the earth and the other five planets revolved around the sun, Lyra laughed loudly at the joke.

However, she was keen to show that she did know some things, and when Mrs Coulter was telling her about electrons, she said expertly, "Yes, they're negatively charged particles. Sort of like Dust, except that Dust isn't charged."

As soon as she said that, Mrs Coulter's dæmon snapped his head up to look at her, and all the golden fur on his little body stood up, bristling, as if it were charged itself. Mrs Coulter laid a hand on his back.

"Dust?" she said.

"Yeah. You know, from space, that Dust."

"What do you know about Dust, Lyra?"

"Oh, that it comes out of space, and it lights people up, if you have a special sort of camera to see it by. Except not children. It doesn't affect children."

"Where did you learn that from?"

By now Lyra was aware that there was a powerful tension in the room, because Pantalaimon had crept ermine-like on to her lap and was trembling violently.

"Just someone in Jordan," Lyra said vaguely. "I forget who. I think it was one of the Scholars."

"Was it in one of your lessons?"

"Yes, it might have been. Or else it might've been just in passing. Yes. I think that was it. This Scholar, I think he was from New Denmark, he was talking to the Chaplain about Dust and I was just passing and it sounded interesting so I couldn't help stopping to listen. That's what it was."

"I see," said Mrs Coulter.

"Is it right, what he told me? Did I get it wrong?"

"Well, I don't know. I'm sure you know much more than I do. Let's get back to those electrons…"

Later, Pantalaimon said, "You know when all the fur stood up on her dæmon? Well, I was behind him, and she grabbed his fur so tight her knuckles went white. You couldn't see. It was a long time till his fur went down. I thought he was going to leap at you."

That was strange, no doubt; but neither of them knew what to make of it.

And finally, there were other kinds of lesson so gently and subtly given that they didn't feel like lessons at all. How to wash one's own hair; how to judge which colours suited one; how to say no in such a charming way that no offence was given; how to put on lipstick, powder, scent. To be sure, Mrs Coulter didn't teach Lyra the latter arts directly, but she knew Lyra was watching when she made herself up, and she took care to let Lyra see where she kept the cosmetics, and to allow her time on her own to explore and try them out for herself.

Time passed, and autumn began to change into winter. From time to time Lyra thought of Jordan College, but it seemed small and quiet compared to the busy life she led now. Every so often she thought of Roger, too, and felt uneasy, but there was an opera to go to, or a new dress to wear, or the Royal Arctic Institute to visit, and then she forgot him again.

When Lyra had been living there for six weeks or so, Mrs Coulter decided to hold a cocktail party. Lyra had the impression that there was something to celebrate, though Mrs Coulter never said what it was. She ordered flowers, she discussed canapés and drinks with the caterer, and she spent a whole evening with Lyra deciding whom to invite.

"We must have the Archbishop. I couldn't afford to leave him out, though he's the most hateful old snob. Lord Boreal is in town: he'll be fun. And the Princess Postnikova. Do you think it would be right to invite Erik Andersson? I wonder if it's about time to take him up…"

Erik Andersson was the latest fashionable dancer. Lyra had no idea what "take him up" meant, but she enjoyed giving her opinion none the less. She dutifully wrote down all the names Mrs Coulter suggested, spelling them atrociously and then crossing them out when Mrs Coulter decided against them after all.

When Lyra went to bed, Pantalaimon whispered from the pillow:

"She's never going to the North! She's going to keep us here for ever. When are we going to run away?"

"She is," Lyra whispered back. "You just don't like her. Well, that's hard luck. I like her. And why would she be teaching us navigation and all that if she wasn't going to take us North?"

"To stop you getting impatient, that's why. You don't really want to stand around at the cocktail party being all sweet and pretty. She's just making a pet out of you."

Lyra turned her back and closed her eyes. But what Pantalaimon said was true. She had been feeling confined and cramped by this polite life, however luxurious it was. She would have given anything for a day with her Oxford ragamuffin friends, with a battle in the Claybeds and a race along the canal. The one thing that kept her polite and attentive to Mrs Coulter was that tantalizing hope of going North. Perhaps they would meet Lord Asriel. Perhaps he and Mrs Coulter would fall in love, and they would get married and adopt Lyra, and go and rescue Roger from the Gobblers.

On the afternoon of the cocktail party Mrs Coulter took Lyra to a fashionable hairdresser's, where her stiff dark blonde hair was softened and waved, and her nails were filed and polished, and where they even applied a little make-up to her eyes and lips to show her how to do it. Then they went to collect the new dress Mrs Coulter had ordered for her, and to buy some patent-leather shoes, and then it was time to go back to the flat and check the flowers and get dressed.

"Not the shoulder-bag, dear," said Mrs Coulter as Lyra came out of her bedroom, glowing with a sense of her own prettiness.

Lyra had taken to wearing a little white leather shoulder-bag everywhere, so as to keep the alethiometer close at hand. Mrs Coulter, loosening the cramped way some roses had been bunched into a vase, saw that Lyra wasn't moving and glanced pointedly at the door.

"Oh, please, Mrs Coulter, I do love this bag!"

"Not indoors, Lyra. It looks absurd to be carrying a shoulder-bag in your own home. Take it off at once, and come and help check these glasses…"

It wasn't so much her snappish tone as the words "in your own home" that made Lyra resist stubbornly. Pantalaimon flew to the floor and instantly became a polecat, arching his back against her little white ankle-socks. Encouraged by this, Lyra said:

"But it won't be in the way. And it's the only thing I really like wearing. I think it really suits –"

She didn't finish the sentence, because Mrs Coulter's dæmon sprang off the sofa in a blur of golden fur and pinned Pantalaimon to the carpet before he could move. Lyra cried out in alarm, and then in fear and pain, as Pantalaimon twisted this way and that, shrieking and snarling, unable to loosen the golden monkey's grip. Only a few seconds, and the monkey had overmastered him: with one fierce black paw around his throat and his back paws gripping the polecat's lower limbs, he took one of Pantalaimon's ears in his other paw and pulled as if he intended to tear it off. Not angrily, either, but with a cold curious force that was horrifying to see and even worse to feel.

Lyra sobbed in terror.

"Don't! Please! Stop hurting us!"

Mrs Coulter looked up from her flowers.

"Do as I tell you, then," she said.

"I promise!"

The golden monkey stepped away from Pantalaimon as if he were suddenly bored. Pantalaimon fled to Lyra at once, and she scooped him up to her face to kiss and gentle.

"Now, Lyra," said Mrs Coulter.

Lyra turned her back abruptly and slammed into her bedroom, but no sooner had she banged the door shut behind her than it opened again. Mrs Coulter was standing there only a foot or two away.

"Lyra, if you behave in this coarse and vulgar way we shall have a confrontation, which I will win. Take off that bag this instant. Control that unpleasant frown. Never slam a door again in my hearing or out of it. Now the first guests will be arriving in a few minutes, and they are going to find you perfectly behaved, sweet, charming, innocent, attentive, delightful in every way. I particularly wish for that, Lyra, do you understand me?"

"Yes, Mrs Coulter."

"Then kiss me."

She bent a little and offered her cheek. Lyra had to stand on tiptoe to kiss it. She noticed how smooth it was, and the slight perplexing smell of Mrs Coulter's flesh: scented, but somehow metallic. She drew away and laid the shoulder-bag on her dressing-table before following Mrs Coulter back to the drawing-room.

"What do you think of the flowers, dear?" said Mrs Coulter as sweetly as if nothing had happened. "I suppose one can't go wrong with roses, but you can have too much of a good thing… Have the caterers brought enough ice? Be a dear and go and ask. Warm drinks are *horrid*…"

Lyra found it was quite easy to pretend to be light-hearted and charming, though she was conscious every second of Pantalaimon's disgust, and of his hatred for the golden monkey. Presently the doorbell rang, and soon the room was filling up with fashionably-dressed ladies and handsome or distinguished men. Lyra moved among them offering canapés or smiling sweetly and making pretty answers when they spoke to her. She felt like a universal pet, and the second she voiced that thought to herself, Pantalaimon stretched his goldfinch-wings and chirruped loudly.

She sensed his glee at having proved her right, and became a little more retiring.

"And where do you go to school, my dear?" said an elderly lady, inspecting Lyra through a lorgnette.

"I don't go to school," Lyra told her.

"Really? I thought your mother would have sent you to her old school. A *very* good place…"

Lyra was mystified until she realized the old lady's mistake.

"Oh! She's not my mother! I'm just here helping her. I'm her personal assistant," she said importantly.

"I see. And who *are* your people?"

Again Lyra had to wonder what she meant before replying.

"They were a count and countess," she said. "They both died in an aëronautical accident in the North."

"Which count?"

"Count Belacqua. He was Lord Asriel's brother."

The old lady's dæmon, a scarlet macaw, shifted as if in irritation from one foot to another. The old lady was beginning to frown with curiosity, so Lyra smiled sweetly and moved on.

She was going past a group of men and one young woman near the large sofa when she heard the word *Dust*. She had seen enough of society now to understand when men and women were flirting, and she watched the process with fascination, though she was more fascinated by the mention of Dust, and she hung back to listen. The men seemed to be scholars; from the way the young woman was questioning them, Lyra took her to be a student of some kind.

"It was discovered by a Muscovite – stop me if you know this already –" a middle-aged man was saying, as the young woman gazed at him in admiration – "a man called Rusakov, and they're usually called Rusakov Particles after him. Elementary particles that don't interact in any way with others – very hard to detect, but the extraordinary thing is that they seem to be attracted to human beings."

"Really?" said the young woman, wide-eyed.

"And even more extraordinary," he went on, "some human beings more than others. Adults attract them, but not children. At least, not much, and not until adolescence. In fact, that's the very reason –" his voice dropped, and he moved closer to the young woman, putting his hand confidentially on her shoulder – "that's the very reason the Oblation Board was set up. As our good hostess here could tell you."

"Really? Is she involved with the Oblation Board?"

"My dear, she *is* the Oblation Board. It's entirely her own project –"

The man was about to tell her more when he caught sight of Lyra. She stared back at him unblinkingly, and perhaps he had had a little too much to drink, or perhaps he was keen to impress the young woman, for he said:

"This little lady knows all about it, I'll be bound. You're safe from the Oblation Board, aren't you, my dear?"

"Oh, yes," said Lyra. "I'm safe from everyone here. Where I used to live, in Oxford, there was all kinds of dangerous things. There was gyptians – they take kids and sell 'em to the Turks for slaves. And on Port Meadow at the full moon there's a werewolf that comes out from the old nunnery at Godstow. I heard him howling once. And there's the Gobblers…"

"That's what I mean," the man said. "That's what they call the Oblation Board, don't they?"

Lyra felt Pantalaimon tremble suddenly, but he was on his best behaviour. The dæmons of the two grown-ups, a cat and a butterfly, didn't seem to notice.

"Gobblers?" said the young woman. "What a peculiar name! Why do they call them Gobblers?"

Lyra was about to tell her one of the blood-curdling stories she'd made up to frighten the Oxford kids with, but the man was already speaking.

"From the initials, d'you see? General Oblation Board. Very old idea, as a matter of fact. In the Middle Ages, parents would give their children to the church to be monks or nuns. And the unfortunate brats were known as oblates. Means a sacrifice, an offering, something of that sort. So the same idea was taken up when they were looking into the Dust business… As our little friend probably knows. Why don't you go and talk to Lord Boreal?" he added to Lyra directly. "I'm sure he'd like to meet Mrs Coulter's protégée… That's him, the man with grey hair and the serpent-dæmon."

He wanted to get rid of Lyra so that he could talk more privately with the young woman; Lyra could tell that easily. But the young woman, it seemed, was still interested in Lyra, and slipped away from the man to talk to her.

"Stop a minute… What's your name?"

"Lyra."

"I'm Adèle Starminster. I'm a journalist. Could I have a quiet word?"

Thinking it only natural that people should wish to talk to her, Lyra said simply, "Yes."

The woman's butterfly-dæmon rose into the air, casting about to left and right, and fluttered down to whisper something, at which Adèle Starminster said, "Come to the window-seat."

This was a favourite spot of Lyra's; it overlooked the river, and at this time of night, the lights across on the south bank were glittering brilliantly over their reflections in the black water of the high tide. A line of barges hauled by a tug moved upriver. Adèle Starminster sat down and moved along the cushioned seat to make room.

"Did Professor Docker say that you had some connection with Mrs Coulter?"

"Yes."

"What is it? You're not her daughter, or something? I suppose I should know –"

"No!" said Lyra. "Course not. I'm her personal assistant."

"Her personal assistant? You're a bit young, aren't you? I thought you were related to her or something. What's she like?"

"She's very clever," said Lyra. Before this evening she would have said much more, but things were changing.

"Yes, but personally," Adèle Starminster insisted. "I mean, is she friendly or impatient or what? Do you live here with her? What's she like in private?"

"She's very nice," said Lyra stolidly.

"What sort of things do you do? How do you help her?"

"I do calculations and all that. Like for navigation."

"Ah, I see… And where do you come from? What was your name again?"

"Lyra. I come from Oxford."

"Why did Mrs Coulter pick you to –"

She stopped very suddenly, because Mrs Coulter herself had appeared close by. From the way Adèle Starminster looked up at her, and the agitated way her dæmon was fluttering around her head, Lyra could tell that the young woman wasn't supposed to be at the party at all.

"I don't know your name," said Mrs Coulter very quietly, "but I shall find it out within five minutes, and then you will never work as a journalist again. Now get up very quietly, without making a fuss, and leave. I might add that whoever brought you here will also suffer."

Mrs Coulter seemed to be charged with some kind of anbaric force. She even smelled different: a hot smell, like heated metal, came off her body. Lyra had felt something of it earlier, but now she was seeing it directed at someone else, and poor Adèle Starminster had no force to resist. Her dæmon fell limp on her shoulder and flapped his gorgeous wings once or twice before fainting, and the woman herself seemed to be unable to stand fully upright. Moving in a slight awkward crouch, she made her way through the press of loudly talking guests and out of the drawing-room door. She had one hand clutched to her shoulder, holding the swooning dæmon in place.

"Well?" said Mrs Coulter to Lyra.

"I never told her anything important," Lyra said.

"What was she asking?"

"Just about what I was doing and who I was, and stuff like that."

As she said that, Lyra noticed that Mrs Coulter was alone, without her dæmon. How could that be? But a moment later the golden monkey appeared at her side, and, reaching down, she took his hand and swung him up lightly to her shoulder. At once she seemed at ease again.

"If you come across anyone else who obviously hasn't been invited, dear, do come and find me, won't you?"

The hot metallic smell was vanishing. Perhaps Lyra had only imagined it. She could smell Mrs Coulter's scent again, and the roses, and the cigarillo-smoke, and the scent of other women. Mrs Coulter smiled at Lyra in a way that seemed to say, "You and I understand these things, don't we?" and moved on to greet some other guests.

Pantalaimon was whispering in Lyra's ear.

"While she was here, her dæmon was coming out of our bedroom. He's been spying. He knows about the alethiometer!"

Lyra felt that that was probably true, but there was nothing she could do about it. What had that Professor been saying about the Gobblers? She looked around to find him again, but no sooner had she seen him than the commissionaire (in servant's dress for the evening) and another man tapped the Professor on the shoulder and spoke quietly to him, at which he turned pale and followed them out. That took no more than a couple of seconds, and it was so discreetly done that hardly anyone noticed. But it left Lyra feeling anxious and exposed.

She wandered through the two big rooms where the party was taking place, half-listening to the conversations around her, half-interested in the taste of the cocktails she wasn't allowed to try, and increasingly fretful. She wasn't aware that anyone was watching her until the commissionaire appeared at her side and bent to say:

"Miss Lyra, the gentleman by the fireplace would like to speak to you. He's Lord Boreal, if you didn't know."

Lyra looked up across the room. The powerful-looking grey-haired man was looking directly at her, and as their eyes met he nodded and beckoned.

Unwilling, but more interested now, she went across.

"Good evening, child," he said. His voice was smooth and commanding. His serpent-dæmon's mailed head and emerald eyes glittered in the light from the cut-glass lamp on the wall nearby.

"Good evening," said Lyra.

"How is my old friend the Master of Jordan?"

"Very well, thank you."

"I expect they were all sorry to say goodbye to you."

"Yes, they were."

"And is Mrs Coulter keeping you busy? What is she teaching you?"

Because Lyra was feeling rebellious and uneasy, she didn't answer this patronizing question with the truth, or with one of her usual flights of fancy. Instead she said, "I'm learning about Rusakov Particles, and about the Oblation Board."

He seemed to become focused at once, in the same way that

you could focus the beam of an anbaric lantern. All his attention streamed at her fiercely.

"Suppose you tell me what you know," he said.

"They're doing experiments in the North," Lyra said. She was feeling reckless now. "Like Dr Grumman."

"Go on."

"They've got this special kind of photogram where you can see Dust, and when you see a man there's like all light coming to him, and there's none on a child. At least not so much."

"Did Mrs Coulter show you a picture like that?"

Lyra hesitated, for this was not lying but something else, and she wasn't practised at it.

"No," she said after a moment. "I saw that one at Jordan College."

"Who showed it to you?"

"He wasn't really showing it to *me*," Lyra admitted. "I was just passing and I saw it. And then my friend Roger was taken by the Oblation Board. But –"

"Who showed you that picture?"

"My Uncle Asriel."

"When?"

"When he was in Jordan College last time."

"I see. And what else have you been learning about? Did I hear you mention the Oblation Board?"

"Yes. But I didn't hear about that from him, I heard it here."

Which was exactly true, she thought.

He was looking at her narrowly. She gazed back with all the innocence she had. Finally he nodded.

"Then Mrs Coulter must have decided you were ready to help her in that work. Interesting. Have you taken part yet?"

"No," said Lyra. What was he talking about? Pantalaimon was cleverly in his most inexpressive shape, a moth, and couldn't betray her feelings; and she was sure she could keep her own face innocent.

"And has she told you what happens to the children?"

"No, she hasn't told me that. I only just know that it's about Dust, and they're like a kind of sacrifice."

Again, that wasn't exactly a lie, she thought; she had never said that Mrs Coulter herself had told her.

"*Sacrifice* is rather a dramatic way of putting it. What's done is for their good as well as ours. And of course they all come to Mrs Coulter willingly. That's why she's so valuable. They must want to take part, and what child could resist her? And if she's going to use you as well to bring them in, so much the better. I'm very pleased."

He smiled at her in the way Mrs Coulter had: as if they were both in on a secret. She smiled politely back and he turned away to talk to someone else.

She and Pantalaimon could sense each other's horror. She wanted to go away by herself and talk to him; she wanted to leave the flat; she wanted to go back to Jordan College and her little shabby bedroom on Staircase Twelve; she wanted to find Lord Asriel –

And as if in answer to that last wish, she heard his name mentioned, and wandered closer to the group talking nearby with the pretext of helping herself to a canapé from the plate on the table. A man in a bishop's purple was saying:

"… No, I don't think Lord Asriel will be troubling us for quite some time."

"And where did you say he was being held?"

"In the fortress of Svalbard, I'm told. Guarded by *panserbjørne*, you know, armoured bears. Formidable creatures! He won't escape from them if he lives to be a thousand. The fact is that I really think the way is clear, very nearly clear –"

"The last experiments have confirmed what I always believed – that Dust is an emanation from the dark principle itself, and –"

"Do I detect the Zoroastrian heresy?"

"What *used* to be a heresy –"

"And if we could isolate the dark principle –"

"Svalbard, did you say?"

"Armoured bears –"

"The Oblation Board –"

"The children don't suffer, I'm sure of it –"

"Lord Asriel imprisoned –"

Lyra had heard enough. She turned away, and moving as quietly as the moth-Pantalaimon, she went into her bedroom and closed the door. The noise of the party was muffled at once.

"Well?" she whispered, and he became a goldfinch on her shoulder.

"Are we going to run away?" he whispered back.

"Course. If we do it now with all these people about she might not notice for a while."

"*He* will."

Pantalaimon meant Mrs Coulter's dæmon. When Lyra thought of his lithe golden shape she felt ill with fear.

"I'll fight him this time," Pantalaimon said boldly. "I can change and he can't. I'll change so quickly he won't be able to keep hold. This time I'll win, you'll see."

Lyra nodded distractedly. What should she wear? How could she get out without being seen?

"You'll have to go and spy," she whispered. "As soon as it's clear we'll have to run. Be a moth," she added. "Remember, the *second* there's no one looking…"

She opened the door a crack and he crawled out, dark against the warm pink light in the corridor.

Meanwhile, she hastily flung on the warmest clothes she had

and stuffed some more into one of the coal-silk bags from the fashionable shop they'd visited that very afternoon. Mrs Coulter had given her money like sweets, and although she had spent it lavishly, there were still several sovereigns left, which she put in the pocket of the dark wolfskin coat.

Last of all she packed the alethiometer in its black velvet cloth. Had that abominable monkey found it? He must have done; he must have told her; oh, if she'd only hidden it better!

She tiptoed to the door. Her room opened into the end of the corridor nearest the hall, luckily, and most of the guests were in the two big rooms further along. There was the sound of voices talking loudly, laughter, the quiet flushing of a lavatory, the tinkle of glasses; and then a tiny moth-voice at her ear said:

"Now! Quick!"

She slipped through the door and into the hall, and in less than three seconds she was opening the front door of the flat. A moment after that she was through and pulling it quietly shut, and with Pantalaimon a goldfinch again, she ran for the stairs and fled.